Jessica's Jo

and

Climate Change

by

Julie Manners

DEDICATION

I would like to dedicate this book to my friends and family,

particularly to my sons

Kevin and Paul

and

to their children

Chantelle, Madison, Ruby

and Jordan

PROLOGUE

The story covers life in general. However, climate change is the principal factor.

Hopefully, in some small way, it may help to enlighten readers with regard to global warming and climate change.

The trail of devastation and destruction we humans have done, and are continuing to do to our planet is, sadly, creating catastrophic disasters worldwide.

PART ONE

Chapter 1

Jessica Aries had left her comfortable home in Bath to attend University to study English and History there. It was beyond her comprehension how but she'd managed to be accepted at one of the Universities in Oxford. Her parents were very proud of her and always wonderful and supportive to both herself and her younger sister Holly. They'd had a happy childhood always taught right from wrong and to care for others. However, it was now time for her to branch out on her own with her parents blessing. Jess made a number of friends at University which helped her and her friends not to miss their families quite so much. It was an exciting time for her and close friends too being grown up and able to manage their lives independently. Jessica, however, did miss her parents and sister and endeavoured to return home to visit from time to time.

A little apprehensive as she left everything and everyone she knew, Jessica was totally aware at her young age this is what she must do so off to University she did go.

It wasn't long before she got to know several students, all in the same boat as her of course. Fresher's week, so named for young people to interact and get to know one another was a great opportunity for them, most having left their comfortable and secure homes for the first time.

One's academic calendar is usually light for the first week, so it was a good time to get to know the campus which could be a rather confusing place. So during her first week Jess explored to figure out where her classes would be, so as not to get lost when they started.

Also this gave Jess time to sort out which societies she would like to join. There were many to choose from but she had for some time been interested and mesmerised in climate change and saw that there was a Greenpeace society so

1

immediately joined up. This is where she met Josie who would become a very dear friend.

Feeling a little vulnerable at first Jess soon felt better about her new independence. Fairly quickly, Jess got to know Josie really well. Well enough to go and explore together between their studies.

When time allowed they managed to take a coach from Oxford and visited Bath Abbey together which both girls found extremely interesting. The Abbey founded in the 7th century was a good starting point for them as they were keen history fanatics. Jess had never had the opportunity before as her parents always seemed to take her and her sister Holly to other cities to explore. Jess, however, had been in touch with her mother who'd invited them both for dinner before they returned by coach to Oxford with their return tickets.

Josie thought Jess's parents were so welcoming to her and hugely pleased to see their daughter even if for a brief visit. Jess with her friend Josie tucked into the wonderful spread before them. Jess's mother, Grace had really gone to town to feed them up before they left. Over dinner her parents listened to their antics and the happy time they were having. All too soon it was time for them to leave. With tears in her eyes Grace and Jess's father Ted bid them farewell and hoped it wouldn't be too long before they saw them again. It was not far for them to walk to catch their return coach, so there was no need for Jess's father to drive them to their coach stop.

Jess's aim in life was to do very well with her studies, find a fulfilling job, explore more on climate change and, hopefully, one day find the right young man to settle down with. Of course this was all in the future and now was the time to study and to take one day at a time.

Both girls were extremely attractive and nice, polite young ladies so obviously got noticed from time to time by young men, either on the same course or out and about as a group. Jess was rather tall with a lovely slim figure with naturally, almost blond, fair hair. Josie, on the other hand, was equally tall with a flattering figure and fairly dark and beautiful natural wavy hair.

2

It was quite some time after Jess's trip to Bath with Josie when a student she'd met at the Greenpeace Society, John from Scotland, asked if she would like to accompany him to the Roman Baths. Oh my goodness Jess thought she'd not that long ago been back to Bath with Josie. On that occasion though they had time only to visit the Abbey as they had spent some considerable time with her parents.

Somehow he must have known that was her home town and quite possibly thought it might be a good idea for her to visit and possibly meet up with her parents too. Yes she was fairly interested in the Roman Baths so agreed and arranged a day when both were free at the same time.

John was a first year student too so both were living in the same halls of residence which, apparently, was when he'd first noticed Jess. He'd had his eye on her for some time but she didn't appear to show much interest in him or indeed anyone of the opposite sex. Jess, of course, was too deeply engrossed in her studies and climate change to notice handsome young men and, of course, not really interested in courtship of any kind at this stage in her life.

However, Jess agreed to go along with John as she too was interested in exploring the Roman Baths. They arranged to meet just after lunch and off they walked to the Bus for their journey to Bath. John did his best to make conversation with Jess who found it rather difficult to understand his broad Scottish accent. She felt she didn't know him well enough to ask him to keep repeating himself and thought it might seem rather rude of her to do so. Anyway she managed to get the gist of whatever he said.

Both John and Jess were consumed with the vastness and history of the Baths, noting when the Baths were built by the Romans. The Romans used the 1.3 million litres of naturally-heated water that rose to the surface spontaneously each day. The Baths combined healing with leisure and water was channelled through the Baths using lead pipes and lead lined channels. Even the Baths were lead lined. People would come from far and wide to bathe in the waters and worship at the temple.

3

The water at the Baths fell as rain on the Mendip Hills many hundreds or even thousands of years ago. It percolated deep down through limestone aquifers, heated by the earth's core and raised the temperature to between 64-96 degrees. Under pressure the heated water rose to the surface at 46 degrees along fissures and faults through the limestone beneath Bath.

During the exploration of the Roman Baths John did take Jess's hand, she allowed him to do so but wasn't that keen as Jess was not interested in John in a romantic way at all, just a nice friend and the last thing she wanted was to lead him on in any way. He seemed to make it obvious that he'd like to get to know her a lot better and, possibly in a romantic way. So no way could she visit her parents this time for fear of .giving John the wrong impression. Jess did feel rather mean as he had been such a chatty and friendly guy to be with, but there was no spark there for her even if she'd been open for romance.

While at University Jess had a few encounters in this way but really not interested at this stage in her life for amorous liaisons. Her friend Josie felt the same way and occasionally would have discussions between them on the issue. Josie did, however, start to date a second year student for some time and was rather taken with him but it did fizzle out towards the end of their student days.

Chapter 2

After finishing her 3 year History and English degree course, Jess decided to take a further year to study Teacher Training. Her future at last she could see teaching primary school children. With her caring nature and her love of children she felt this was what she was destined to be, a teacher of young ones.

Initially Jess would probably have returned to her parents' home to live, but now some-what matured and having enjoyed caring for herself, this she felt was not now an option for her.

Jess remained in her bedsit from studying days and wanted to remain in Oxford where she had been to College and also completed her Teacher Training Course. She loved Oxford and the friends she'd made and most were staying on in the same vicinity.

Jess with her close college friend Josie, now lodged together and would be in close proximity over the next couple of years with odd jobs like waitressing, and child minding in order for them to have the opportunity to travel before they settled down with the permanent jobs they intended to do in the future. However, they were in no great hurry and found their new found freedom most enjoyable.

In the meantime out for their usual walk over the meadow where they chatted about the possibility of being able to afford a special holiday together. Where to go, they were unsure but maybe somewhere abroad. It was beautifully quiet on this April morning when both derived pleasure letting their gaze wander over the expanse of grounds beautifully cultured. Josie and Jess enjoyed the attractive layout of the grasses with the abundance of mature shrubs and conifers giving a feeling of serenity. Enhanced by this warm spring morning with the singing of the birds and the perfume of buds just beginning to blossom heightened their thoughts to get away.

So deeply consumed as they chatted together about several destinations as to whether or not they could actually afford to go. However, they finally agreed that Hawaii, surrounded by beautiful islands, would be a grand place to visit before they settled down into their permanent jobs, which they both must find sooner or later.

'I have a cousin who works for one of the major airlines', explained Josie 'I'll try and find out from her if she has a way of knowing the cheapest way to get there'. 'Oh that's great' said a now excited Jess 'I will do some research myself to find a suitable and economic place for us to stay'.

They both agreed to do this initial task before they made their final decision as to whether or not they can actually afford to embark on this rather exotic holiday.

Over the next few days this is all the girls can talk about. Josie contacted her cousin and Jess did her research for a suitable place to stay.

Shortly thereafter home from their work shifts, which are at odd times as usually the girls are not home at the same time so seldom are together to catch up. Waitressing was not an ideal job for either of them, but found work in a high class hotel paid them a little more money and, they believed, the tips were a lot better than working in a Restaurant. It did mean, though that their shifts were separate from each other which wasn't too beneficial when they, at times, had a need to be together, especially to discuss their possible holiday. Occasionally when Jess arrived home from her shift, Josie would be in bed fast asleep and the same with Jess when Josie arrived home.

Now for a brief period of time they excitedly sat down together before duty called. 'I managed, eventually, to get hold of my cousin Danielle, who I'd forgotten to tell you is Dutch said Josie and continued. 'Danielle said as soon as we can let her know if and when we would like to travel she would arrange flights for us to fly standby'. 'That means we go to the Airport and take the first flight that has two available seats'. Jess then asked 'does that mean we could get on a flight immediately or we could be waiting for hours?' 'Yes, I'm afraid that is exactly what it means', Josie retorted.

They weighed up the pros and cons and eventually agreed that this, by far, was the cheapest route to take then both nod in unison that this is what they should do.

6

'Have you managed to find some reasonable and economical accommodation?' questioned Josie. 'Yes, I have' said Jess. 'It's a 3 star hotel, a twin room with bed and breakfast only and it is fairly cheap'. 'Excellent' responded Josie.

They both felt it must now be all systems go for this wonderful holiday to Hawaii, but must work out some kind of itinerary before they make their absolute final decision.

Firstly, both decide to work extra hours to build up their bank balance in anticipation for their most exciting trip.

Chapter 3

Just two months after many discussions as to whether or not they could afford to take such a holiday, the girls find themselves at the Airport awaiting their flight to Hawaii. Josie had been told by Danielle that there would be two flights on this particular day and to get to the airport fairly early. The first flight would be leaving at 1000am so they arrived before 6 o'clock, a very early start for them. They were amazed to be called for this, the first, flight as there happened to be two available seats. Well if this was standby it was pretty good as far as they were concerned.

After a long 17 hour flight, where they managed to at least catch up on their sleep during the journey, they arrived in Honolulu to a beautiful and sunny climate. The wonderful warm and balmy air engulfed them as they descended the plane steps and headed through to the arrivals lounge. After which they found a taxi to transport them to their Hotel in Waikiki, not too far from the airport and relatively inexpensive.

Now at their hotel and after they'd checked in, Jess said she would take their luggage up to their third floor room via the lift. Josie, however, would not use the lift as it made her claustrophobic which meant she would have to climb the three flights of stairs to their room. Jess failed to understand this but if that was what Josie preferred to do that was fine with her.

Jess found their room fairly easily which looked rather comfortable with two single beds, teas-making facility and a bathroom with bath and a shower. Jess had unpacked and wandered about for some considerable time, made a cup of tea and began to wonder where Josie had got to. She'd chosen a bed and relaxed for what seemed some long while when she heard the door open. 'Where on earth have you been?' Jess said in a concerned manner. 'You may well ask' Josie responded. 'I walked up three flights of stairs and found the door locked at the top. Down I trundled had to find and explain to the concierge who gave me a key to unlock the door. So up the three flights again and here I am at last'. 'Oh poor you, sit down I'll get you a nice cup of tea' said Jess. 'Yes, thanks, I could really do with that, I'm so hot now' gasped Josie.

It's now early morning for them but having slept on the plane the night before they do not feel at all tired at the moment. The girls had picked up some leaflets from the hotel and studied what they should do and where they might venture on their first trip out.

However decide to have a quiet day and find a supermarket to buy some lunch. They locate a Safeway just ahead of them and pop in for their lunch snack and walk to the beach nearby and relax. Spreading their towels on the sand they settle down to eat their sandwich and drink their bottled water. The sea is a heavenly sky blue with bathers and a few people water skiing. Everything looked so idyllic. Jess and Josie agreed how wonderful to be here looking up at the clear sky and absorbing the warmth of the glorious sun.

They'd relaxed for some time when Jess said 'come on let's take a stroll along the beach'. Josie was all for it so together they wandered along the shore and came across a number of small Restaurants. One in particular looked wholesome and not too expensive so decided to come back later, have an early dinner there, and go to bed and catch up on their sleep after the long journey, also to work out a plan for the following day.

The girls were back at their hotel after a very early light dinner to work out their finances to last over the 10 days. 'Shall we go to Turtle Bay tomorrow' questioned Jess as both looked through the hotel brochures of what to do and where to go. 'Well I think we should' Josie retorted 'the tours look rather expensive though, perhaps we could go by bus, what do you think?' 'Yes', producing a bus brochure, 'I'm sure there should be a number of buses going to Turtle Bay' suggested Jess.

After both had studied the brochure information they chat about the fact that there are two types of turtles, the green sea turtles and also one called the Hawksbill sea turtle. They read that it is illegal to touch the sea turtles and to keep at least 15 feet away. 'Oh that's a pity' Josie remarked 'I would at least like to be a little closer than that wouldn't you?' 'Yes I would too, must be difficult for people who are really short-sighted' Jess responded with a grin.

Between them, as they lay on their separate twin beds, find a bus service and decide to get up very early the next morning to take the bus to Turtle Bay.

The girls had made arrangements the night before with the hotel staff to have a very early breakfast before departing north to The Bay.

The bus arrived at the scheduled time with not too many passengers aboard but the girls deduced they were all mainly tourists. It was a lovely journey the bus stopped off at various places and waited for them. The first stop was alongside a Macadamia Nut Farm where there were many flavours to choose from and one could try the samples, and all for free. This really suited Jess and Josie as they had to watch their finances. There were many flavours that were so delicious. As they returned to the bus both girls expressed how exceedingly grateful they were to the bus driver as he'd waited for them.

Not far along the road from the Nut Farm they saw an island that looked like a hat. Also known by locals as Chinaman's Hat because of it's shape, which the driver, on his intercom, explained.

Native Hawaiian flowers all around, together with ferns are spotted on their journey to the Bay. Many wonderful sites were passed but their focus was now on Turtle Bay. All too soon they arrived. The driver expressed a time for their return journey and both girls again uttered their thanks to the driver as they alighted from the bus.

Across the road from where the bus had stopped, such a beautiful sight before them of a wonderful almost white sandy beach. Not too many tourists there either. There were a number of green turtles lazing on the sands. Apparently the sea turtles crawled up onto the warm sands to take a nap.

Very carefully Jess and Josie approached the beach and kept well away from the turtles, but really cannot take their eyes off of them. Getting as close as they dare and having done a little research can see that they are mainly green sea turtles as they possess a teardrop shaped shell. This is called a carapace, which is the shell structure, and they have a pair of large, paddle-like flippers. The girls also found out that, very interestingly, the shell of the turtle has nerve endings, which meant they can feel if touched and it hurts them when their shell is damaged.

As they looked around they were unable to see any Hawksbill turtles which are distinguished from the green sea turtle by its curving beak with a prominent cutting edge, and the saw-like appearance of its shell markings.

Totally mesmerised by these sea creatures, Jess and Josie find a quiet spot on the beach, not too far away from the turtles, and just stare at them. 'Oh if only we could get a little closer' said Jess not able to remove her eyes from them. 'Yes' her friend responded 'If only we were allowed to be closer, I would love to stroke them, but we're not. We will have to take pleasure in watching them from a few feet away'.

They spent the whole afternoon lazing on the beach with the many sleeping turtles. Well they appear to be sleeping. After what seemed an age there is movement when one moves, then another and another until they all trundled back into the water. Jess and Josie mesmerised just gazed at them. They'd only seen a tortoise back home, but these turtles were really so large and gorgeous. Jess took a photo of this wonderful army of turtles as they trundled back into the Bay, which is where they find their food, so they must have been a little hungry after their sleep.

The girls had already eaten their sandwich bought from the Supermarket the day before, so decide to take a paddle in the Bay. Jess is not a good swimmer, although Josie is. However, she is a little dubious about going for a swim for fear she may come too close to the turtles.

While both paddled, the turtles are pretty close to them. Obviously used to humans take no notice of them or anyone else at all.

A number of people are now in the water and wondered if they could possibly be snuggled up to the many turtles as it was rather difficult to keep the required 15ft away.

Now back in their spot on the beach they lie out on their beach towels again and take in the warmth of the afternoon sun excitedly chatting about these wonderful creatures.

It is now time to wander over for their return bus trip. Wait no more than 10 minutes when the bus duly arrived. A fairly long bus ride but the girls felt it worth every moment.

It is fairly late when they eventually arrive back to their hotel so dumped their things then decide to try some local food for supper. There are a few food shops dotted about so it doesn't take too long and end up with fish tacos.

The next day decide to stay local after their fairly long trip to Turtle Bay. After a little more research find beautiful Hawaiian flowers and learn that the Hawaii State Flower is the Yellow Hibiscus, a delicate beauty, meaning unity and peace, a perfect representation of Hawaii apparently.

Flower colours are diverse on the Island of Maui which include, white, orange, yellow, pink, salmon and purple hybrids as they contain combinations of all of these colours. The flowers are well known for their use in making flower Leis. These beautiful and fragrant flowers can also be worn in the hair by women to indicate their relationship status. Worn over the right ear if single and over the left if taken. 'Oh we learn something every day' said a smiling Jess.

Jess and Josie, both interested in history, would like to visit Pearl Harbour as earlier they'd looked over the information. They both decide the cheapest way to get there is again by bus.

Both very much looked forward to this venture and after a rather long bus ride, arrive at Pearl Harbour. The first thing they notice at this very large and informative Museum is '*ATTACK ON PEARL HARBOUR*'. Pictures of the devastation before them 'goodness how absolutely dreadful for those poor servicemen with no warning of what was about to happen to them' exclaimed Josie. With a nod of her head and with an utter look of sadness Jess agreed. Then both began to read the many placards:

'The attack was a surprise military strike by the Imperial Japanese Naval Air Service upon the United States (a neutral country at the time) against their Naval Base at Pearl Harbour in Honolulu, Territory of Hawaii, just before 8 o'clock on Sunday morning, December the 7th, 1941 The attack led the United States formal entry into WW2 the next day.

The attack commenced at 7.48 am Hawaii time (18.18 gmt). The Base was attacked by 353 Imperial Japanese aircraft (including fighters and dive bombers, also torpedo bombers) in two waves launched from six aircraft carriers.

Of the eight US Navy battleships present all were damaged, with four sunk. All but USS Arizona were later raised, and six were returned to service and went on to fight in the war.

The Japanese also sank or damaged three cruisers, three destroyers, an anti-aircraft training ship, and one minelayer. A total of 188 US aircraft were destroyed, 2,403 Americans were killed and 1,178 others were wounded.

Japanese losses were light: 29 aircraft and 5 midget submarines lost, and 64 servicemen killed. The Commanding Officer of one of the sub-marines was captured.

Japan announced declaration of war on the United States and the British Empire later that day, but the declarations were not received until the following day.

There were numerous historical precedents for the unannounced military action by Japan for the lack of any formal warning.

US President Franklin D Roosevelt proclaimed December 7th 1941 "a date which will live in infamy".

Because the attack happened without a declaration of war and without explicit warning, the attack on Pearl Harbour was later judged at the Tokyo Trials to be a War Crime.

'Oh my goodness how dreadful this must have been for those poor souls, their families must have been devastated back home when they heard the terrible news of their loved ones' Jess remarked and Josie just nodded grim faced in agreement.

Just before leaving they noticed the reason why the Japanese went to these lengths of devastation. The Japanese objective was to prevent the US Pacific Fleet from interfering with their conquest to capture Southeast Asia.

Jess and Josie came away with the thought that it was extremely moving and also very interesting, but a sorrowful, place to visit.

They moved on and found the exact spot on the Ship USS Missouri where on the 2nd September 1945 the formal surrender of Japan to the Allied Powers was signed, thus bringing to a close the Second World War.

To see the names on the plaque inscribed "To the memory forever of the gallant men entombed here and their shipmates who gave their lives in action on December 7th 1941 on the USS Arizona". The girls were almost in tears before they departed.

After their few exhaustive trips, money began to get rather low so the girls spend the latter days of their holiday with long walks in the sunshine and lazed on the beach. Josie, of course, would often take a dip in the sea while Jess watched and paddled in the warm water.

With 3 days left it was now nearing the end of their glorious holiday so the girls decided to spend the afternoon on the Beach, read their books and watch the sunset later. They had heard about the wonderful sunsets so both agreed it would be lovely to witness it themselves.

Take a brief walk then head off to the beach with hats, sunscreen and a good book. They occupy a deck chair each it was rather nice to have a relaxed afternoon from their many exhausting ventures as they intend to remain until sunset.

However, there were a number of people on the beach with surfers in the sea, but they were able to close their minds to the goings on and read their books in relative comfort.

Such a delightful afternoon with the warm rays of the sun shining down, the happy sounds of little children nearby and occasionally watched the surfers having fun. From time to time the girls would observe but were thoroughly engrossed in their books too.

Suddenly they looked up at what seemed a commotion by the water's edge. A small girl in a dingy appeared to be in distress being swept out to sea with difficulty to get back to the shore.

Both Jess and Josie dropped their books and stood to get a better view. The water now not quite so calm, a young man waded out to sea in desperation to try to help her. He too was finding it extremely difficult with the current pushing him away from where he was attempting to reach the frightened child. After some time he managed to reach her, although the dingy had overturned before he could get to her and had thrown her into the water.

Both now extremely alarmed at what was happening before their eyes, ran to the water's edge but stood back not wanting to obstruct the rescue. The brave man managed to grab the young girl and keep her head above water and fought hard against the current to swim back. By this time Lifeguards had arrived to help him and the child out of the water.

'Oh my goodness I do hope they're ok' said Josie. They could see that there were two Lifeguards one with the young man and one with the girl pumping water from their lungs. They looked pretty lifeless until there was a cough and a splurge from each of them in turn. The little girl started to cry uncontrollably which was a good sign when they noticed the rescuer give a weak smile that she was ok. The crowd who'd stood around to watch gave them a loud cheer for what they'd done. Were then wrapped in blankets and taken away to recover from their ordeal. The girls could see a distressed woman nearby who must have been the child's mother. 'Oh thank goodness' said Jess as they returned to their deckchairs.

Now able to tuck into the goodies brought along for their early supper before the sun started to set.

It wasn't too long after this escapade that the sun was now beginning to set, which was the reason they had stayed on the beach for so long.

With the stunning hues of the sunset before their eyes was a dramatic introduction to the finale of a day well spent with the reflection of the shimmering ocean as palm trees swayed gently in the slight breeze. Josie captured the stunning colours as they danced across the skyline before the sun began to sink beyond the horizon. 'That was incredibly amazing to watch' Jess remarked. 'Oh I'm so glad we stayed to witness it' said Josie. What an incredible day retorted the girls as they wandered over to their hotel.

Jess thought they should do one more exploration of the island before their departure home. So agreed between them and decided to visit the Hawaiian Volcano Observatory as their homeward journey would be the day after tomorrow. They'd spent 3 days walking the beach, taken in the sights and lazed with their books now for their last adventure before they packed up to leave.

Jess and Josie had saved their money by embracing the local food. For instance the locally caught seafood and tropical fruits and the sparkling pineapple wine so delicious and refreshing on a hot day.

It was fairly easy to find a bus route that went directly to the Centre, as this was the cheapest way, as usual, to get them to the site.

The first information they came across was that the Hawaiian Islands were formed by the intermittent outpouring of lava from the floor of the Pacific Ocean.

Heat from a relatively stationary hot spot deep within the earth's mantle created magma or molten rock that rose through the overlying pacific plate and erupted on the ocean floor.

After thousands of eruptions, an island is built like a rocky mass above sea level.

The plate subsequently moved over the hot spot and created a succession of islands in the Hawaiian Ridge.

The Hawaiian Islands are but mere tops of gigantic mountains rising from the floor of the ocean. The island of Hawaii was formed by 5 volcanoes but only 3 are active; Hualalai, Mauna Loa and Kilauea. The latter two are the world's most active volcanoes.

The Hawaiian Islands remained isolated from the rest of the world until Captain Cook in 1779 sighted the islands which he called the Sandwich Islands after the Earl of Sandwich, also known as John Montague.

The English navigator returned to discover the islands in the main group, including Hawaii. He was killed by Hawaiian Warriors while anchored at Kealakekua Bay on the Island's West Coast. A monument marks the spot. That reminded Jess of a saying she'd heard "Whatever you wish to do be the best that you can. Leave your mark!" Well Captain Cook certainly had.

'Oh my goodness, that was a fair amount of historic information to absorb' said Josie. 'Yes, I wouldn't be a bit surprised if the English Government sent him to sail around the world to commandeer uninhabited islands and look what happened to him' Jess exclaimed. Both girls found the volcanoes extremely interesting, particularly as they erupted fairly frequently.

Much of the Observatory's observation is on Kilauea and Mauna Loa, as they are significantly more active, which is why most of their concentration is on these two volcanoes. Mauna Loa is the largest active volcano on Earth. Kilauea is presently one of the most productive volcanoes on Earth (in terms of how much lava it erupts each year).

Since 1952 Kilauea has erupted many times. Eruptions of Kilauea are certainly spectacular. Its cherry-red lava flows and roaring lava fountains are impressive, especially when seen at night. However, relatively few people have been killed by its lava, because it is usually possible for people to get out of its path.

The one major fatality at Kilauea was caused by a steam explosion. In 1794, lava-heated groundwater killed a troop of soldiers marching past the caldera (a large hollow that formed shortly after the emptying of a magma chamber in a volcanic eruption which can cause a sudden release of gas). But such explosions at Kilauea are rare.

As they make their way back to the bus for their hotel, the girls chat away on their findings with regard to the Hawaiian volcanoes.

In need of some rest and relaxation before their journey home, the girls decided to spend the next couple of days at the beach as it was only a short walk from their hotel. As they sauntered along with their beach towels listened to bird song with the sun a bright shining crimson, it was heavenly. Extremely lucky to go to their secluded part of a little bay as they'd heard on arrival the beach can be very busy with surfers from around the globe. Further along on the North Shore the surfers apparently come to ride the huge suicidal looking waves that can occasionally pound the shore line.

How blessed the girls thought they were to find this secluded little bay when they first arrived. Whilst lazing on the sands it was rather wonderful to feel the warm breeze and to smell the fresh ocean water. 'This is like paradise for us' remarked Jess. 'Oh I so agree with you, we will miss this so much' Josie retorted

Before their usual lunch Josie decided to go for a quick swim as Jess watched enviously as she paddled in the shallow water. Apart from a few young children, as they searched for sea shells, everything was so peaceful. Their parents lazed quietly with a beady eye on their little ones.

Chapter 4

The time had come for their departure. Packed up the night before, took their final breakfast checked out of the hotel then left for the Airport. 'Let's hope our travel home will be as easy as when we left' said Jess. 'Yes, I'm sure all will be fine' Josie responded. Both girls happily assumed there would not be a problem as, of course, there hadn't been from London to Hawaii as standby passengers.

Unfortunately, they were forced to wait all day and all night as there were no flights available with vacant seats for them.

They began to get extremely tired and alarmed both girls afraid they could be here at the Airport for days and felt very despondent. With just enough money for a sandwich and a drink both realised that they must be careful as they had no idea of how long they would have to wait for a flight to London.

After 36 hours they were called but the flight would take them to Los Angeles only. Both girls thought that that would be a step in the right direction and decided to take it.

Now most concerned wondered just how long they would have to wait at Los Angeles for a connecting flight to London, but at least they were on their way home albeit only half way.

As they arrived in Los Angeles, Jess and Josie both felt extremely tired, unwashed and desolate. They nipped into the Ladies Cloakroom to splash their faces and wash their hands when Josie said 'I'm going to telephone this guy Bruce who is a friend of Danielle's family, I know his surname so, hopefully I can find his number in the telephone book'. Jess was so tired she really couldn't absorb what Josie said.

As they left the Ladies Room, Jess found a seat unaware that Josie had found this guy Bruce's number and had obviously nodded off while Josie made the telephone call.

Josie shook Jess by the shoulder 'wake up Jess, Bruce is coming to collect us'. Sleepily and really not caring now Jess managed to ask 'what happened?' 'I successfully got through on the telephone and Bruce answered, I explained as quickly as I could what had happened to us'. 'Bruce's response was well what do you want me to do?' Josie continued 'I really was unsure what to say to that, so Bruce said 'we're having a dinner party tonight for University friends and two guests cannot make it so I'll pick you up at the Airport and you both can stay for dinner'.

Oh my goodness was Jess's first thought she felt so very tired and couldn't think of anything worse.

Josie dragged Jess out of the Airport to await Bruce's arrival. Within a very short time this man, named, Bruce arrived. Jess climbed into the back of his car after a brief welcome and tried her best not to fall asleep. She could hear the drone of Bruce and Josie's voices but not heeding a word of what was said as she gazed out of the window now and again and thought they were headed into an extremely salubrious neighbourhood.

The car pulled into a fairly long driveway before Bruce stopped beside a beautiful house. Oh my goodness Jess began to think, here they were having not slept or washed for some considerable time being invited to have dinner with people she had not the faintest idea as to who they were.

They were greeted at the door by Bruce's wife Harriet, a most wonderful and friendly lady. 'Do come in girls, I'm so sorry to hear of your plight but you are most welcome to have dinner with us tonight'. Jess's eyes brightened at this most motherly and friendly welcome.

Harriet took them through the hallway and spacious sitting room and asked if they would like to have a quick wash before dinner as their other two guests were due to arrive very soon. 'Thank you so much that would be lovely' said Jess and continued in her sleepy state 'I do hope we're not causing you too much trouble, it's so very kind of you to include us in your dinner party like this'.

Taking them through to a huge bathroom Harriet continued 'Oh we're so pleased to have you. I believe Bruce mentioned two of our guests are unable to make it this evening, so you are more than welcome'.

Each given a clean towel alongside the bathroom Harriet left with the words 'Oh I can hear our two other guests have arrived so when you've finished please join us for a drink before dinner, you'll hear where we are by our excited chatter. 'Thank you so much' said Josie.

The bathroom was very large with two sink basins so they didn't mind being alongside one another to have a very quick wash. The bathroom was really beautiful with gold taps, the sinks and surrounds in a gorgeous flecked marble. Quickly looked around saw the huge bath also surrounded with the same marble, the very large shower too. They realised, of course, that they must be very quick as the other guests had arrived. The girls remained in the same clothes as there was so little time to ferret through their cases to change.

Josie managed to say quickly to Jess that she would explain later how she had heard of Bruce but, hurriedly said, would do so as soon as possible.

Heading in the direction of voices they found the four of them stood together with a drink in their hand. Bruce stepped forward and introduced them to their guests and visa-versa.

Asked what they would like to drink, both Josie and Jess plumped for a non-alcoholic drink.

The other two guests were Molly and Ken, two University friends of Bruce. After a quick acknowledgement of each other they were then ushered into the Dining Room.

Oh my goodness thought Jess as they entered as she looked at the most sumptuous table setting, so colourful and beautifully laid out. At each place there were two plates a large one with a smaller one on top, a white linen napkin splendidly folded resting on the plate with a sparkling cut glass to the side.

Harriet seated at one end of the table with Bruce at the other end asked Jess to sit alongside her to her left. Josie was seated opposite to Jess with Ken next to her and Molly next to Jess. Very well organised as each couple were opposite to each other.

Apparently the dinner party had been arranged to discuss events happening at the University. However, they were just desperate to hear everything about Josie and Jess's Hawaiian holiday.

Whilst enjoying the most magnificent dinner, and between mouthfuls, the girls did their level best to explain what they had seen and done. Jess livened up and really enjoyed the splendid company of everyone. Harriet touched Jess's hand at the end of the meal and said 'I'm sure you are so very tired you must go to bed now'. Jess's immediate reactive thought was she had no idea that they would be staying there the night. In fact due to tiredness had paid little thought to exactly what or where they might be going after dinner.

Harriet continued 'I'll show you both to the bedroom'. Jess felt overcome with gratitude as she stood up from the table. With that Josie remarked 'Jess look behind you'. Jess turned around and saw that the blinds were open whereupon she could see that they were high up. It was extremely dark with many sparkly lights and in huge letters the word '**HOLLYWOOD**' splayed out down below. Jess just gasped with surprise. As she'd had her back to the window with no idea of what was behind her.

Jess revealed her delight and surprise at just how magnificent it all looked. The girls said how wonderful it was to meet the guests before saying an extremely thankful goodnight before Harriet guided them through to the bedroom. 'Harriet, this is immensely kind of you and Bruce to let us stay, I really don't know how we can ever thank you enough' said a terribly tired Jess. 'Oh we are very pleased to have you' Harriet responded with a kindly smile.

Shown into a double bedroom with two single beds, Harriet gave them each a white dressing gown and said she hoped they slept well and would see them in the morning. Jess couldn't help but give Harriet a huge hug and the biggest thank you for being so amazingly kind.

Both had a quick wash and dived into bed. Although tremendously tired Jess couldn't wait to hear how Josie had come to know this extraordinary wonderful couple. She started with 'Danielle's grandparents, in Holland during the war, who found Bruce with two other American soldiers hiding from the Germans. They were very young, boys really, so Danielle's grandparents hid them for many weeks. Of course they were taking a terrible risk, if the Germans had found them hiding their enemy they would have been shot. The young soldiers were cared for with food and clothes during this period. Josie had also been told that, at the time Bruce had conveyed he hoped one day to repay Danielle's Grandparents for their kindness. Josie guessed, in a way, he could be repaying the kindness given to him all those years ago by taking us, two stranded travellers into his home'.

Jess listened intently to Josie's explanation 'what a wonderful story' said Jess and immediately fell asleep.

Awakened by bird song the girls felt so much better after their longed for sleep. They'd had only a quick wash the night before and fallen into bed totally exhausted. Each took a quick, and very welcome shower, dressed and headed through the house together. 'Good morning girls, I would have brought you a cup of tea in bed but thought it best not to wake you' said Harriet. 'Thank you' said Josie 'but we're as bright as a button this morning after a much needed wonderful sleep'. 'Yes, thank you so much' Jess reiterated.

They sat down together for breakfast during which Bruce said 'I've been in touch with your airline this morning and, after explaining your situation, was told there would not be two seats available standby for three days. That does mean you will be stuck with us'.

To hear this statement from Bruce Jess felt rather alarmed, and thought of poor Bruce and Harriet stuck with them as he'd gracefully announced.

'Oh I'm so sorry' remarked Jess 'we really don't wish to be a burden to you both and feel so bad when you've welcomed us so sincerely already into your home'.

Harriet then remarked 'believe me Jess, we are most delighted, our own family live a fair distance away and won't be visiting until later next month so it is a joy for us to have you'. 'Thank you so very much' said a gleeful Josie with a graceful nod from Jess.

'Right, said Bruce 'we're going to take you both for a ride out to Beverley Hills, does that appeal?'

Jess open mouthed couldn't express her delight more deeply which could not have been made more obvious to Harriet and Bruce at both girls deep pleasure with the mere thought.

Later, they motored through palm tree lined streets, home to the rich and famous. Bruce passed many beautiful gated properties, the crown jewel of Los Angeles County. Most had rather long driveways, which sadly made it quite impossible to view the fearfully expensive homes.

Bruce and Harriet appeared to take great delight as they showed the girls around. To hear their excited joyous gratitude as they watched the electric fountain come alive with varying lights and water patterns. Bruce asked if they'd ever seen this particular fountain before as this specific fountain had made appearances in several films. Of course they hadn't.

They were then taken to The Beverley Hills Hotel to reflect on the luxurious ambience of this amazing hotel. Jess and Josie felt like celebrities in another world as they walked through the red carpeted foyer, took a seat for a short while just to admire in disbelief their beautiful surroundings.

To capture a perfect souvenir, Harriet suggested she take a photo of them in front of the famed Beverly Hills sign in Beverly Gardens Park fairly close to the hotel.

On to Rodeo Drive, Bruce noticed the girls shear excitement as he drove along this world famous Rodeo Drive. There were so many designer shops: like Gucci, Amani, Coco Chanel, Cartier and many more. The design of every shop was incredibly amazing.

Bruce asked if the girls would like him to stop to look inside some of the shops. 'Thank you but no thank you' the girls said in unison. Jess continued 'we'll leave the shopping to the rich and famous'. Knowing full well they were completely out spent and nothing could be worse than viewing something very special they couldn't even envisage to purchase.

Now way passed lunch time Bruce pulled into a small Café well away from the main Rodeo Drive and all went inside for a quick snack lunch.

Both Jess and Josie were extremely conscious that they had very little money so both opted for a small sandwich with a glass of water. Bruce tried his utmost for them to choose something more appetising, but they insisted on the sandwich but he did persuade them to change the water for a cup of coffee.

By now it was late afternoon so time to retreat home. The girls were wholeheartedly thankful to Bruce for a wonderful exploratory day out and both helped Harriet in the kitchen to prepare supper.

Their second night in this lovely home with the two most adorable people, Jess and Josie couldn't find enough expressive words of delight to one another before going off to sleep.

At breakfast the following morning Bruce with his pleasant tone of voice said 'well girls I think Harriet and I will take you to Venice Beach today as, hopefully, you may fly home tomorrow'. 'That would be most exciting thank you so much' said a gleeful Jess 'I know of Venice in Italy but nothing of Venice Beach in LA'. Bruce then went on to say that Venice Beach was founded in the early 20th century by a tobacco millionaire and developer from New Jersey who wanted to build a replica of Venice, Italy – his favourite city – but in America as a themed seaside resort along the Pacific Coast Road.

The wealthy businessman dreamed of creating a fabulous city modelled on Venice, Italy. Many of the streets in Venice, Los Angeles, were once canals. Initially there were very many to recreate the appearance and the feel of Venice, Italy. However, when cars gained more popularity a lot of the canals were filled in to make roads so there are only about four canals left now.

They left Bruce and Harriet's home to explore Venice Beach together. Jess continued to be mesmerised by the friendliness and the incredible hospitality of these two loving people.

After Bruce had managed to park the car, his advice was that they first of all explored the Venice Canals which would show a completely different side to the beachfront later. The four of them took a stroll through three canal-lined blocks of an Avenue – hence the name Venice – where they discovered an idyllic scene: arching pedestrian bridges, charming beach houses, bunches of ducklings and the occasional paddle boarder.

After absorbing the Venice Canals they strolled along to the beachfront, Jess walked beside Harriet and Josie with Bruce as it was a fairly busy bustling scene with skaters as they passed on the Promenade. Along the walkway with its parallel bike path there were many pumped up gym enthusiasts doing their workouts, with many T shirt stands as they sold their wares.

Jess and Josie just gawped at everything they saw when a breathtakingly and beautiful girl passed by. She wore a rich green silk dress with a high buttoned front with an A line skirt which reached down to just above her shapely knees. The matching jacket, nipped in at the waist, was a perfect combination with the dress. Both girls immediately thought she must be a famous actress as she strolled along with an equally well dressed young man. Of course Jess and Josie were very casually dressed in jeans and T-shirt covered with an attractive cardigan, Jess in pink and Josie in green. Most of their clothes still packed away required laundering.

Off they then strolled to the Farmer's Market where there were a conglomeration of food booths and so much to see. In front of their eyes was a round pool with a magnificent fountain spilling water in various shapes around the pool with stunning architecture and designer shops nearby.

Obviously Jess and Josie thought it was just a food market with a name like Farmer's Market so both were astonished to see so many different wonders. To them it was like being in a fairyland.

They'd walked around for some considerable time, the girls still open-mouthed in absolute awe of it all, Bruce broke their thoughts with 'I think it's time to have a bite to eat, are you hungry?' 'Yes rather' Josie responded.

Bruce seemed to know his whereabouts in this very bustling and busy market place and led them off to a Food Booth where they had the most fantastic Veggie Grill Burger which was most delightful and filling.

By now they'd walked for several hours so Jess thought of poor Harriet and asked if she was ok. Harriet responded that she was and had thoroughly enjoyed the look of appreciation on the girls' faces. So now it was time to head back to Bruce and Harriet's home.

The time with this truly remarkable couple was now drawing to a close. The next day they were due to fly home to the UK.

There was an air of sadness around the room, particularly from Jess and Josie but also quite obvious from Harriet and Bruce also. This amazing couple had put themselves out to accommodate two stranded girls was above and beyond kindness.

Their final supper was cooked by the two girls but first required Harriet's permission who had agreed. However, they were rather shy to poke around to find what to cook so Harriet kindly showed them the fish and vegetables that had been delivered earlier in the day. Jess sensed that Harriet seemed a little uncomfortable with the girls loose in her kitchen, principally because she was the host. Jess with her arm around Harriet's shoulder said 'You have taken care of us, now it's such a small thing we can do in return. Josie and I can cook reasonably well, and we're very good at clearing up so please go and relax with Bruce'. 'Ok, if you're sure' and with a smile Harriet turned around and walked from the kitchen.

The girls put their heads together, with quiet discussion, as to how they were going to present a really acceptable and tasty dinner. Both had insisted Harriet and Bruce rest up, the girls worked out just how they were going to cook a, hopefully, delicious, supper with the salmon, vegetables and potatoes before them.

Josie said she would first deal with the salmon. Found an oven proof dish after switching the oven on to 160c, she proceeded to prepare the fish by brushing each piece with olive oil and seasoning well with salt and pepper. Jess had already peeled a few potatoes to boil and to lightly fry before placing in a dish with seasoning to bake in the oven. Then together they prepared the broccoli spears and green beans.

Pudding would be easy as it was blueberries and raspberries with ice cream.

Within less than an hour the girls were ready to dish up. The salmon looked beautifully cooked and succulent, the potatoes lightly fried and baked with seasoning looked crisp but light and the vegetables retained their glossy green colour.

'Shall we take the dishes into the Dining Table for everyone to help themselves' said Josie 'I don't think so replied Jess 'why don't we plate everything up and quickly wash up the dishes beforehand'. 'Good idea' said Josie. The food did in fact look rather professional they agreed as they walked into the Dining Room with two colourful plates each. As they placed them down Bruce spoke first 'Oh this looks rather scrumptious'. 'Yes, it does thank you girls' said a gleeful Harriet.

Jess and Josie were rather pleased, as they'd worked together in a strange kitchen and were able to produce a very nice, edible supper. Insistent to clear away the dishes they, of course, left the kitchen in immaculate order.

All retired to bed fairly early after a delightful chatty evening together, as tomorrow would be the end of their marvellous time with this charming and wonderful couple.

A rather subdued breakfast together was taken the following morning before their departure to drive to Los Angeles Airport. It was rather incredible but Harriet and Bruce were allowed to accompany the girls' right up to the aircraft. All four were extremely solemn at the thought of saying goodbye. Jess spoke first with gentle tears falling down her cheeks 'We can never thank you enough for the care you've given us. We're sure you will leave footprints on our hearts forever'. Josie nodded in agreement, also with eyes watering and added 'we'll never forget you and truly hope that one day we'll see you again. Though many miles may be between us, you will never be far from our hearts'.

As tears flowed they all hugged and kissed, the girls boarded the plane. Turned with one final look at their new found friends and with a final wave disappeared inside the aircraft.

The girls felt so sad at leaving dear Bruce and Harriet looked out of the plane window souring through the summery skies into the fleecy clouds and had a rather subdued but uneventful flight home. During their journey they reminisced on their remarkable holiday and their phenomenal three days with Harriet and Bruce.

After a short film, a cabin meal and a nap they had landed at Heathrow and in no time were home.

Chapter 5

Now recovered from their exciting holiday the girls were rather desperate to secure permanent jobs and settled down with some urgency to do so. They had, of course, looked into this before departure for their holiday.

It was not long before Josie had an interview for her longed for Forensic Assistant post at Police Headquarters. Jess on the other hand had a couple of interviews for teaching Primary School children.

Of course the time also arose for both to find more salubrious accommodation which they felt was the right time to do this too, which obviously made absolute sense. So between job interviews the girls trotted off separately to look up various Estate Agents. 'Good luck, see you later' they bellowed to each other as both turned in opposite directions.

They'd lived in the same lodgings for some considerable time so had agreed, provided they were not too far apart from one another, it wouldn't be catastrophic if both lived separately. Josie would forever be Jess's best friend from their college days, whatever.

After their accommodation search, Josie had been very successful and appeared to have pipped Jess at the post when she announced she'd been taken to view the flat she would like. As they chatted together to discuss other options Jess said she hoped to look over a couple of flats and told Josie where they were situated. 'Oh that's only a couple of miles from the one I'm interested in' Josie with glee expressed. The girls are extremely pleased with their eventful day as they'd explored estate agents and hoped to reach a happy conclusion.

Josie received a telephone call in the morning from Police Headquarters that she'd been offered the post as a Forensic Laboratory Assistant and to report to Police HQ to commence employment in a week's time. A letter would be in the post for confirmation in a day or so. Jess heard her cry of excitement from the bedroom and tore down the stairs to see what it was about 'I've been offered the job I dearly wanted Jess, I'm so excited'. 'Well done 'ole girl' and Jess immediately gave her dear friend a huge hug.

Jess had previously found a school where, if possible, she would most like to teach. And had, shortly before their holiday, made contact with her preferred school and was anxious to hear from them. She had expressed in her letter that she would be unavailable for some two weeks due to her holiday if, by any chance, there was a possibility for her to be called for interview.

Two days later Jess is astonished and happy to receive a telephone call from the school with a request for her to come for interview in 10 days'. This is such good news for Jess as, hopefully, she will be settled into her new home before her interview at the school she preferred for employment.

Jess had looked on line and through local Estate Office windows previously so knew exactly where to find nearby and appropriate Estate Agents. She had called in on a couple of them and asked questions about possible flat vacancies but to no avail. The third one she'd found, she'd called into their office and after relevant questions had decided to return the following day to view a few flats that were available, whereby appointments would have been made to look them over..

'Good morning, I'm Jessica Aries' she greeted the Receptionist. 'Good morning' was the reply 'You have an appointment with Derek Jones' and picked up the telephone and called him from another office.

'Hello, how are you?' greeted Derek Jones as he walked towards her and shook Jess's hand. 'I'm fine, thank you'. 'First of all I'd like to show you photos of two flats and where they are located. If you like them I'll take you in my car to view them if that's ok with you'. 'Yes, fine' Jess responded 'but obviously I'd like to see where they are first'. 'Of course' said Derek.

As she studied the photos Jess could identify exactly where one in particular was situated, which is near to the school where she has an interview in a few days and, hopefully, eventually employed. Both flats look rather similar so Jess is interested in both, one a little further away from the school.

'Right' said Derek 'I'll take you to view both flats, but before I do I'd like to explain that the one you are most interested in is a shared house. A young lady lives there, but you'd be completely independent from each other. You'd use the same outer door just that the young lady has the upper part of the house and you would have the lower, is that ok with you?' Jess thought about it for a second and replied 'Yes, I think so but I would like to see the house and also meet the young lady before I make my final decision, if possible'.

So Jess climbed into Derek Jones' car the properties only a short distance away from his office. Derek pulled the car alongside the flat, and Jess cast her eye around. She thought it rather nice and a pleasant location but a little too expensive for her pocket. Just a little further away was the shared house Jessica was most interested in. Also it was only a short distance away from the school where she hoped, against hope, soon to be working.

Jess could see it was a rather large house divided into two flats. Entering through the doorway she noticed the stairs to the left but Derek ushered her through the small hallway. To the right a large bedroom, then further down the hallway a small kitchen and a large living room. It did look really nice and very cosy. Also there was a pretty garden with a lawn and a few flower borders. 'Would I be responsible for maintaining the garden' questioned Jess. 'No' responded Derek 'the Landlord does see to the garden on a regular basis'. Jess thought that's good, she could sit in the garden during the summer months and not have to maintain it.

Jess viewed the flat and the garden and as she expressed her thoughts to Derek on their way out all of a sudden they heard someone as, whoever it was, bounded down the stairs 'Hello, how do you do, I'm Claire from the flat upstairs'. Jess, was taken by surprise and could see that Claire was slightly younger and possibly a little high spirited. Derek responded first gave his name then introduced Jess to her. 'Oh I do hope you come' said Claire 'it would be comforting to know that someone else is living here for company'.

'Yes, nice to meet you' said Jess 'I have to weigh up a few things before I make a decision, but hope to see you again'. Derek Jones and Jess then left the flat and returned to his office to listen to Jess's comments.

Back in his office Jess was shown to a seat to discuss with Derek her thoughts on the two flats. A welcome cup of tea was brought over by the kindly Receptionist. 'Thank you so much' said a grateful Jess.

As they went through everything together, Jess was extremely happy to take on the shared accommodation. Although she and the other tenant, Claire, would be completely separate which, of course, was Jessica's preference.

Arrangements were made for Jess to move in as soon as she was ready. It was, therefore, agreed that she would move in the following week.

Jess excitedly explained to Josie that she would move out in a week's time and gave her the address of the flat she would shortly take up residence. Josie, on the other hand had some good news too, but would not move out for a couple of weeks. This, she said, would enable her to settle things with their landlord before she too departed. Jess thanked Josie implicitly for doing so on her behalf and reiterated what an amazing friend she is and always would be.

During the girls' final week together they have a good clear out. Jess wanted to do as much as possible before she left in order for Josie to have a calm week before she too would leave for her new residence.

Before Jess left both girls put their heads together to compile a truly thankful and constructive letter between them for Bruce and Harriet. To thank them most implicitly for their wonderful hospitality, their kindness and all that they'd done for them. Over the three days with this wonderful couple both expressed how they'd grown extremely fond of them. How Bruce and Harriet had treated them so fondly as if they had been their own daughters. They truly hoped that one day they would be able to visit and repay a little of the kind heartedness that had been shown to them. In the meantime, the girls expressed they would continue to keep in touch with the hope, most sincerely, that they would one day see them again.

Chapter 6

Jess was really excited about the move to her new home. Claire, obviously at home, when Jess turned the key to open her door Claire again bounded down the stairs to greet her. 'Hi Jess, welcome' said Claire. 'Hello again' she replied and thought it very kind to be given such a friendly welcome. 'I'll leave you to settle in' she said then disappeared back up her stairs. Grateful to be alone to sort everything out, Jess got on with the task in hand.

Just a few days later Jess arrived at the school for her interview. She hoped and prayed that she would feel comfortable to work at the school and the Head Teacher and staff would like her enough to accept and employ her.

As she walked through the door of the school Jess was greeted by the School Secretary and asked to take a seat. Jess began to feel a little nervous and apprehensive, sat down as instructed and waited. It wasn't long before a middle aged woman approached her held out a hand to greet Jess said 'Hello, I'm Avril Smith one of the teachers here and will assist at your interview'. 'Hello, nice to meet you' replied Jess as she shook her hand and walked with Avril Smith to the Board Room. Whereupon, Jess was asked to take a seat and greeted by the Headmistress, Mrs Dora Orchard, who introduced her to Mr Peter Johnson, Head of Local Education and John Barlow the Deputy Head.

The room, Jess presumed, was an unused classroom with pictures children must have drawn which covered the walls.

Jess took her seat on one side of the fairly long table, the four interviewers sat opposite which made her feel a little intimidated with four people as they confronted her. Anyway she told herself she must man-up and deal with whatever would be asked of her.

After brief formalities and greetings, Miss Orchard started the proceedings 'Jess would you like to tell us a little about yourself?' Oh my goodness Jess thought briefly, but quickly, I must respond but heck this is not going to be an easy question to answer. These words raced through her mind.

Jess's pause, however, was brief and smiled before she started with her reply. Firstly, she explained about her upbringing, her schooling, then on to university and later how she'd moved on to Teacher Training. Jess continued that she had always felt rather enthusiastic about teaching Primary School children. Had enjoyed University and Teacher Training and, according to her Tutors, had done very well.

Jess continued with 'I have the tenacity, determination and mind-set to be a passionate teacher who, I believe, can adapt under pressure and deliver results'.

The Deputy Head then asked Jess 'would you describe to us your teaching plan?' Jess replied 'I believe in group exercises with class engagement to cater for everyone and to make the material as interesting as possible with slides and videos'. I am an effective communicator with a strong ability to plan ahead and a supportive person. Also I would feel a great sense of achievement to see my class of children develop and grow as individuals'.

'How would you deal with behaviour management'? Mr Johnson asked. Jess replied 'I would set three boundaries. Respect for each other, the right way to respond to ask questions and the way to answer them and, finally, the right way to learn. I feel I am flexible enough to cater for a diverse range of learning skills'.

'How would you deal with the pressures of teaching' asked Avril Smith. Jess replied 'to be aware, and to totally understand the Job Description and for everyone to work together to achieve the aims of the school and the pressures that are placed upon the school'.

'Jessica' Mr Barlow remarked 'Do you have any questions you would like to ask the interview team here?' Jess took a few seconds before she replied. 'Well I don't have any real specific questions, but I believe you are aware I am extremely keen to teach History and General Studies to my pupils. This of, course, would cover many topics which I have planned. I would like confirmation that this would be acceptable'.

34

Miss Orchard replied to her question. 'This was discussed by the team before your interview Jessica and we are all agreed your General Studies teaching would be accepted by this school as, of course, you had presented us with a list of topics of what these would involve. It was also taken on board your interest in climate change'.

'Thank you' said Jessica. Mr Johnson then stood 'I think we must now draw this interview to a close. It has been a pleasure to meet you Jessica. You will be hearing from Miss Orchard in due course as to whether you have been successful'. The other members, together with Mr Johnson shook her hand said their farewells and Jess departed the interview room.

Jess walked back to her flat breathing a sigh of relief that the interview was over. She believed, whatever happened, that she had done as well as she possibly could. However, she desperately hoped well enough to be accepted for the teaching post at that particular school.

Back at her flat it is fairly quiet as Claire is at her workplace as a Hospital Administrator but said she would call in later to ask how Jess had faired with her interview. In the meantime she made a welcome cup of tea for herself, did a few chores then went for a brisk walk.

Jess began her walk through the local meadow, listened to the birds as they chirped away in the breeze. What a wonderful time of year went through her head, also her mind could not escape the interview she'd had earlier. She quite liked the team of people who interviewed her, they appeared rather formal but friendly. Jess hoped with all her heart that they thought she was good enough to employ as she walked on.

Back home prepared to put the kettle on for another cup of tea when there was a knock at her door. Opened the door, stood before her was Claire. Before Jess could say hello, Claire with a smile on her face said 'Hi Jess I thought I'd drop in to ask how you got on today?' 'Hello Claire, would you like to come in and have a cup of tea, I've just put the kettle on'. 'Yes, ok thank you' responded Claire.

Claire's administrative work as Assistant to a Consultant at their nearby very large General Hospital had popped home on her way to take some blood samples to their nearby Laboratory.

So over a cup of tea Jess opened up to Claire about her interview, how she hoped she'd given adequate answers to the questions put to her. That she felt she had but time would tell. Went on to say that she hadn't seen around the school but from her brief visit it looked fine and sincerely hoped she would get employment there. Claire was extremely interested and happy that the interview went well. After a quick cup of tea she bade farewell to Jess and went on her way.

Within a few days Jess received a letter from the school 'Minford Primary' from Miss Orchard. Nervously she scanned the letter and could see that she had, in fact, been offered the teaching post. Her role would be History and General Studies Teacher for years 4 and 5. Miss Orchard would like Jess to contact her at the school to pay a short visit before she joined them to be shown around and to meet other members of staff before her start date.

Jess did a quick dance around her living room thrilled to be given this opportunity. After she'd calmed herself down picked up the telephone and asked to speak with Miss Orchard. After a brief discussion it was arranged for Jess to meet at the school the following day.

As soon as Claire arrived home from work Jess skipped up the stairs, knocked on her door and was immediately beckoned inside. 'By the look on your face, I think you have some exciting news' said Claire. 'Yes' replied a bubbly Jess 'I've been offered the job'. 'Brilliant' responded Claire. They sat down together with a cup of tea when Jess explained all.

It's so nice to have someone like Claire to share things with thought Jess as she returned to her flat. Jess now understood Claire better and believed her to be a genuine, kind and caring person.

After a rather restless night, Jess is eventually woken by the sound of the early morning song of the birds. She scrambled from bed to make a hurried breakfast, took a quick shower before she left for the school.

The school is just a brisk short walk away and again is greeted by the School Secretary who is far less formal this time. 'Hello, my name's Beth, I'll call Miss Orchard for you'. 'Hello again' responded Jess 'thankyou'.

Miss Orchard walked towards Jess with a smile, shook her hand said congratulations and that she very much looked forward to Jess being one of their team. 'If you would like to come with me I'll first show you around the school then take you to meet members of staff who are at the moment free. Those who are busy teaching just now, you can meet later'. 'I'm really looking forward to being shown around' said Jess and also to meet members of staff'.

The school, Jess noticed, is not huge but has an adequate playing field with a small playground. She is shown the Deputy Head's office, John Barlow who is not there and obviously teaching at that moment. Then she is taken to the Staff Room where there are a couple of female teachers having a break with a cup of tea. 'Hello ladies I'd like to introduce you to our new member of staff Jessica Aries who will be joining us next week'. Jess could see that one is probably middle-aged and the other a fair bit younger. The older one approached Jess first. 'Oh so good to meet you I'm Anne Wicks the Maths teacher, I'm sure you will be very happy here'. The younger one then stepped forward 'Hi, nice to meet you I'm Jane Phipps the English Teacher'. Jane then introduced Jess to Pat who is their supply teacher. Jess shook their hands and remarked just how much she was looking forward to joining them at the school next week.

Dora Orchard then took Jess around a number of classrooms. She does not disturb the lessons in progress but took Jess to meet the children she will be teaching. There is a supply teacher with them at the moment. Miss Orchard knocked on the classroom door and entered. Angus Smith, another supply teacher, greeted them and Miss Orchard expressed her apologies and hoped not to have disturbed their lesson. She turned to the children, a class of about 25, and introduced Jess to them. 'Miss Aries is going to be your new teacher for the whole of this year and the following year from next Monday. I hope you will all make her very welcome'. They all appeared to nod in unison. Jess had agreed with Dora Orchard earlier that she would like to have a few words with the children.

'Hello children' said Jess a little nervously. 'I really look forward to be with you all next week. I hope you'll help me to get to know you and to learn your names'. They appeared again to nod in unison. Jess and Miss Orchard then departed the classroom to leave Angus to get on with his lesson.

Before Jess left the school she is taken to the Staff Room again as there should be a few other members of staff there as it is almost lunch time. 'Hello again' she is greeted by John Barlow. 'Would you like some tea? 'Hello, yes please, thank you' replied Jess. There were two other members of staff who approached her and shook her hand after John had done the introduction 'Hello, good to meet you, I'm Sue Davidson the Geography Teacher'. The other person came forward shook Jess's hand 'I'm Philip Gardner the Sports Teacher'. Dora Orchard then declared she must take her leave with the suggestion Jess got to know the other staff members over a cup of tea before she left. Her final comment she very much looked forward to Jess joining the school the following Monday morning.

Phew, Jess thought as she left the school on her way home, that was very informative. She felt all the staff members she'd met had made her feel most welcome. Her focus now must be on preparing her lesson for her pupils with the sincere hope that she will be able to engage with all of the children and get to know each one individually as quickly as possible.

Claire came in to join Jess for a cup of tea a little later when they had a good catch up together on their day's events. They'd now become not just good neighbours but good friends too. It's so nice for them to have each other. Not to feel pressurised, but to feel free to communicate over a cup of tea when neither are work committed. Jess is interested to hear about Claire's job too, as she is Assistant to a Cancer Consultant. She had explained that she worked with a nice happy team, but that it is rather sad when occasionally patients do not respond to treatment so well, but wonderful when they do. Claire mentioned to Jess that she told her boss off one morning when she could see on the Board that a patient had passed away during the night and Claire was saddened by the fact that he appeared somewhat jovial. He told Claire gently but firmly that he would not be able to do his job if he became depressed each time this happened. That he was there to treat and help his patients in any and every way possible. He and his team would continue to do this in spite of the fact that, occasionally, they would sadly lose a patient. Claire said to Jess that she had, of course, to accept his comments and understand that. Jess thought, as Claire did, it must be rather sad at times but that was the job she was in and had undertaken. Jess admired Claire so much for doing her best to understand, and accept, her boss's comments also to understand the patients she came into contact with.

Jess felt that they both could become really good friends, despite having met since she'd moved into the flat. However they appeared to have a lot in common which was good to share on occasion.

Jess had not, as yet, started her job so had more free time than Claire at this moment. Of course with her dear friend Josie over the years and now living separately from one another, it took the little emptiness away at not having her closest friend nearby anymore. Even though they would, of course, keep in touch as frequently as possible.

Chapter 7

Her mobile phone rang; it was her dear friend Josie. Jess had kept her informed of her immediate plans. 'How's everything going?' Josie asked 'Great' responded Jess 'I've just moved in'. 'Oh super, would you like to meet up tomorrow night for supper with a few friends. I thought it would be a good idea before I make my move next week, when I may be a little too busy?' 'Yes be good to see you Josie, miss you already so what's the arrangement?'

'I haven't had the opportunity to tell you but I've bought a little car. I'll pick you up at 7pm from your flat, now you've given me the address and we'll meet the others at Castle's Restaurant on the High Street'. 'Well that's a real nice surprise Josie, wonderful, thanks, will so look forward to it especially seeing you' replied Jess 'but who are the others?' Jess questioned. 'Oh Jeff and Mike' she responded. 'Really nice friendly guys who I met at work'. After their hurried goodbye Jess continued with her sorting out and looked forward to the next evening, although Josie had given her very little information about these two young men. Well, she guessed they were young with very little to go by. However, Jess imagined they were working at the Police Headquarters as Josie did mention she had met them at work which must have brought her into contact with them at some stage. Jess did wonder why Josie had arranged for them to meet up as a foursome. Knowing Josie though, Jess presumed they must be very pleasant guys or she would never have suggested such a thing. Maybe she'd find out a little more over dinner.

True to her word Josie arrived on the dot the following evening the girls so pleased to meet up at last. It seemed an age since they'd seen one another, although really not that long. But such a lot had happened recently and while they'd lived separately. Josie now established in her new job as a young Forensic Scientific Assistant in the Laboratory at the main Police Headquarters, which she'd remarked, brought her into contact with these two men. Now Jess shortly to start her new position as a Teacher. Well it's good to meet up beforehand with new people Jess thought but, most of all, meeting up with her great friend Josie.

After Josie had parked her car, which wasn't so easy, they entered the Restaurant. Josie explained to Jess on the way how she'd come to ask these two guys from work, who were both anxious for a night out having been up to their eyes with surveillance work, studying forensics in the Laboratory and other duties too, but that was as much as she relayed.

Josie had told Jess their names which she had already forgotten and found them stood at the Bar. 'Hi guys, this is Jessica' said Josie as she turned to Jess and continued 'this is Mike' who was the one nearest to her 'and this is Jeff'. Jess a little taken aback by two complete strangers said a cheery 'Hello'. After a quick greeting Mike immediately asked what they'd like to drink. Both girls requested lemonade with lime then walked over to their table quite sure they would be drinking a glass of wine with their meal.

As they settled down at the table, Josie explained to Jess a little of what the three of them had been working on in the Police Laboratory which to Jess sounded extremely interesting and rather exciting. However, she did not reveal in great detail as some matters should, obviously, not generally be talked about. Mike and Jeff, of course, were far more senior than her. Jess guessed they must have signed some Secret Act to not disclose certain aspects of their job to others.

Over dinner Mike conversed with Jess and seemed interested enough to ask what she did. Clearly Josie hadn't told these two men much about her other than a friend from University and that they had shared accommodation. Jess told Mike that she would shortly be starting her new job as a Teacher to 8 and 9 year olds at the school she most wanted to work in. 'Oh good luck when you start' responded Mike. 'Thank you' said .Jess between mouthfuls of watercress soup. 'Can you tell me anything about your particular job' said Jess not really sure what else to say to him as Josie and Jeff were deep in conversation together. Mike explained to Jess that he was a Criminal Detective Investigator which meant the need to work in the Laboratory from time to time and that's where he'd first come into contact with Josie.

Their meals then arrived at the table, Jess and Josie with salmon, en croute, mashed potato and spinach and the men had steak together with chips and peas.

They all chat away together when Jess explained that Josie had told her very little about the two of them. Jeff turned to Jess and commented 'all Josie had said about you was how you'd met each other at college then went on to Teacher Training but you were already firm friends'. Josie, of course as you know, did not end up as a teacher but did a further course on forensics to allow her to be where she is now. Jeff continued 'Josie didn't elaborate too much but remembered she'd said something about a teaching post that's all'. Anyway it's good to put a face to this imaginary person she talked so fondly off'.

Mike then butted in and turned to Jess 'I remember she'd said you had just moved into your new home'. 'Yes, I've just moved into my new flat, well it's shared although we are completely separate from one another' Jess confirmed.

Mike questioned Jess further on what she hoped to teach the children in her class and what she was most passionate about. She explained that she would be teaching mainly History and General Studies which would be anything else generally of her choice. Jess continued 'I hope, when the time is right, to introduce them to climate change and global warming as that is my passion' she emphasised to him. Jess did not go into great detail for fear of boring him so, at this stage, said very little about the subject.

Mike had great eye contact with Jess which, of course, she found attractive as there's nothing worse when one speaks to someone and their gaze is elsewhere. Jess did notice the deep blue of his eyes and his ruffled light blond hair and sharp cheek bones which made him look rather handsome. It was too soon to presume his personality was as good as his looks though.

Jess had, however, detected a little sadness in his deep blue eyes, but perhaps that was because he was not altogether comfortable meeting a stranger for the first time.

After a very nice meal and an enjoyable evening together, both girls insisted on paying for their own meals, it was time for farewells. Jess came away with the thought that Mike and Jeff were really very good company and very pleasant. Not knowing their ages, of course, Jess reckoned they were a few years older than herself and Josie.

'Maybe see you in the morning chaps must just pop Jess home'. Both Mike and Jeff gave Jess a gentle peck on the cheek said how very nice it was to meet her and hoped to see her again sometime.

Back in the car 'I think Mike quite liked you Jess' said Josie 'Oh don't be silly' remarked Jess 'he was just being polite and friendly'. 'Ok, time will tell'. 'Anyway thank you for a lovely evening Josie and for picking me up too in your new car, well new to you. 'That's ok my 'ole friend, we must meet up again soon' then dropped Jess off at home. With a quick wave goodbye Jess unlocked her door and disappeared inside her flat.

Mike had felt a connection with Jess but it had been some long while since he'd had any association with the opposite sex. It was Jeff who'd persuaded him to meet up as a foursome. He'd felt it was time Mike did something pleasurable rather than work.

Jeff had known Mike for a number of years and was well aware of his past, when he had been desperately in love with Lucy. Lucy was a wonderful, pretty and energetic girl and Mike had become engaged to this level-headed, intelligent girl.

They had been engaged for about a year and had looked forward to the months ahead as they planned their wedding day. During this period Lucy became very sick. However, she was exceedingly stoical, convinced that she could and would beat the cancer ravaging her body. Mike loved her all the more for the way she coped and he was there with her every step of the way, right to the end.

Mike had been truly devastated when Lucy lost her fight for life and had, therefore, shut himself away from everyone and from appreciating life himself again. His life over the past couple of years had been dedicated to Lucy's memory and to work, most of all with his surveillance work.

The fact that Jeff had encouraged him to meet up with Josie and her friend was, in fact, rather a blessed miracle that he'd agreed. Josie, of course, was unaware of Mike's past as Jeff had thought it was not his right to divulge this to her, although they had become very good friends.

Mike had felt rather guilty about the connection he'd felt with Jess. Lucy had been his life and his guilt was to her memory. Perhaps he wasn't yet ready to meet someone else.

Chapter 8

A knock on Jess's door, oh that must be Claire she thought. Opened the door yes there was Claire. 'Hi Jess, may I come in' she asked. 'Of course' said Jess. They sat down with a cup of tea together when Claire said. 'I have an afternoon off tomorrow, if you've nothing planned, I wondered if you would like to come with me on a tour of the Oxford Colleges. There's an open topped bus that does regular tours'. 'Oh I'd really like that' Jess replied. So arrangements were made to meet at 2pm the following afternoon.

Jess wasn't due to start her teaching post until the next week so thought it would be a lovely enjoyable distraction. Her life recently seemed to be taken up with interviews and climate change research. It would be a pleasant, educational afternoon out and very much looked forward to it.

Not meeting up until 2pm would give Jess the morning to work on her first lesson for the children she would be teaching.

The tour commenced on the open topped bus at 2.30pm. Jess thought it really rather magical to hear some of Oxford's history. First they passed Oxford Castle where the Bus Courier spoke briefly that William the Conqueror directed Norman Baron Robert D'Oyly to build the castle in 1071 to dominate the town.

The bus then passed Christ Church College which had produced 13 British Prime Ministers. On then to Carfax Tower at 74 feet, no building in central Oxford may be constructed higher than the Tower with 99 steps to the top.

Next was the Radcliffe Camera, built in 1737-1749 and part of the world famous Bodleian Library complex and housed mainly English, History and Theology books. Only students and scholars are admitted.

Then the bus meandered along the streets to Magdalen Bridge and the Botanical Gardens. Here Jess and Claire hopped off the bus to explore the beautiful gardens containing more than 8,000 different plant species.

The Oxford Botanical Gardens are the oldest in Great Britain and one of the oldest scientific gardens in the world. Plants are grown here for medical research. For instance; Cardiology (heart complaints); Oncology (cancer and cell-proliferation); Infectious Diseases (viral and parasitic); Dermatology (skin complaints); Haematology (blood typing and disorders); Pulmonology (lungs and airways) and many others. Jess and Claire were absolutely mesmerised by these factual statements.

They witnessed the Alpine House where plants cannot grow to their full potential outside and are displayed in this House.

The Tropical Lily House where tropical water lilies grow in boxes in a tank. There were too many different plant houses to explore, all growing astounding numbers of plants from around the world.

Again the girls were both captivated and enthralled by what they had witnessed.

Hopped back onto the bus they passed several other Colleges. The oldest University College, Balliol and Merton established between 1249 -1264. The fourth oldest College was Exeter, built in 1314. Both Jess and Claire found this all extremely knowledgeable and rewarding both very interested in history.

Balliol College was founded as long ago as 1263 by John de Balliol. Balliol College has existed as a community of scholars on its present Broad Street site since that date and claimed to be the oldest College in Oxford and in the English speaking world. Boris Johnson studied Classics at Balliol College from 1983 to 1987. However, these were just dates and very ancient buildings which were wonderful to look at and to know roughly when they were built but felt they needed to know more. 'The only way to do that would be to walk around individual colleges at some stage in the future, time permitted' suggested Claire. Jess in agreement hoped they might be able to do that at some stage.

As they alighted from the bus, Jess looked at Claire and said 'Well that was so fascinating'. 'Yes it was, I'm not sure about you, Jess, but it made me really want to know more about one or two of the individual Colleges'. 'Me too' Jess agreed 'as we mentioned earlier let's try and arrange that another time'. They head for home with thoughts on their exploratory afternoon together.

However, they thought their busy work schedules might prevent them from more Oxford College scrutiny in the near future, but would do their level best to fit it in one way or another.

On their walk home the girls reiterated how intrigued they'd been to hear, during their tour, that Hitler intended to use Oxford as his Capital if he conquered England in WW2. This, apparently, was one of the reasons Oxford was not bombed. 'How absolutely dreadful if any of the wonderful, ancient Colleges had been destroyed' expressed Jess.

Chapter 9

On Monday morning Jessica's first day in her new job at Minford Primary School, she arrived ahead of the children and was greeted by other members of staff. The Head teacher, Miss Orchard, welcomed her warmly too. Before Jess was taken to her classroom she explained to Miss Orchard how she intended to approach the children and eventually what her first education lesson would be.

'Very good' said Miss Orchard and accompanied Jess to the classroom. The children had not yet arrived so this gave Jess a little time to adjust herself in readiness for their appearance.

The children trooped in together one after the other and went to their seats in the classroom. They are extremely quiet perhaps a little concerned as to what to expect from their new teacher.

When all are comfortably seated Jess welcomed them with a smile. 'Hello my name is Miss Jessica Aries and I am so pleased to be your 4th and 5th year teacher, which means I will be your teacher for 2 whole years'. Jess continued 'I'm really excited to meet you and to have you all in my class. We are going to have a fabulous school journey with a year full of fun and learning! I'm now going to give each of you a label and I would like you to write your name down on the label and place it onto the front of your jumper. You may then all judge to see how long it will take me to learn and remember all of your names'. Jess beckoned to a girl in the front row who promptly left her desk to stand alongside Jess. 'Hello what's your name' asked Jess. 'My name is Holly' the child answered. 'Ok Holly, that's a pretty name, would you please hand out a label to each child to write their name on, thank you'. While Holly handed them out, Jess said to her class 'I will have a sticky label too with my name, Miss Aries, written in large letters I would like you to write in large letters too'. 'Remember you have only one name to remember, I have 25. So I hope you will all help me'.

Within a few minutes they have their sticky labels on their uniforms for Jessica to read. However, she noticed that one small boy appeared to be struggling so Jess approached him. 'Is it not easy for you to do' she questioned. The little boy nodded and she noticed a few giggles in the class. Jess turned around with a sharp look and asked the child 'what is your name?' 'Tommy' he replied. 'That's a nice name' said Jess and wrote his name on the label and placed it onto his jumper.

'There now we each have a label with our name on. I have made a chart of the classroom and where you are sitting. I'm going to write down your names on my chart, please do not change seats or I will get confused, is that agreed?' 'Yes Miss Aries' they all chanted.

Jess believed it most important for the children to accept who is in charge and to be polite and kind to one another. Also very aware that just one unruly child in a classroom could disrupt everyone else. However, all appeared relaxed and quiet probably as each weighed up their new teacher.

As she'd just met her class of children and not yet had an opportunity to know them by name, thought she'd like to start with a little story for them.

'Right children, as I have said, it is very nice to meet you all and I'm sure by tomorrow I will have learned your names'. 'Now we've all met each other I think you may like the story I'm going to read to you'. I would like you all to listen very carefully because you never know if I may ask you questions at the end'. They appeared to look at Jess with great intent Jess could see in their facial expression, with hope in their eyes, that they might enjoy the story.

'This story is called the Elephant and the Ant' Jess started to read. Once upon a time there lived a huge elephant in the jungle. Because he was so much bigger than all the other animals, he would always trouble them. In the same jungle lived a family of ants. They were a hard working family who always kept themselves to themselves. During the day they would go to gather food when one day the huge elephant threw water all over them. 'Hey what's the matter with you' shouted the ants. 'Why do you keep troubling others?' 'Oh shut up you

tiny ant one word out of you and I will walk all over you'. The ant kept quiet and went on his way.

The ant's mother said to him 'You shouldn't pick a fight with the elephant he is very strong, he's very bad tempered and he could crush you'. 'Something needs to be done to teach him a lesson' said the ant.

So the next day the ant went to the sleeping elephant and climbed into his trunk and started to bite him. 'Ow, ow' cried the elephant as he swished his trunk first left then right to try to dislodge the ant from his trunk. The ant continued to bite him. 'Stop, please stop' the elephant cried. 'Very well' said the ant but only if you stop bothering us'. 'I'm so very sorry, I will never do it again' said the elephant. 'Very well' said the ant again and stopped biting the elephant.[1] 'So you see children you should never pick on anyone who is a little smaller, or not quite as strong as you. Also should you see any of your class mates being pushed or bullied in the playground, it would be kind of you to go to their rescue whoever it is'.

'I was teasing when I said I would ask questions at the end of the story, so no questions just for each of you to understand from the story how a tiny ant was able to overpower a huge elephant'.

'Also how very important it is to be kind and helpful to each other'. I hope this little story will help you to understand'.

Now time for the afternoon session, Jess needed to know how well the children can read. All her pupils have a copy of the book Jess held in her hand. She then proceeded to ask each child, in turn, to recite a page for her. This enabled her to judge how well their reading is, although she is not their English teacher.

Jess is really quite impressed with most of the children. Their reading ability she determined was really very good for their age group. Tommy, however, was somewhat behind, together with Jordan and Oliver. These 3 small boys would require a little extra tuition to catch up, which Jess was determined to do.

Jess was relieved when her first day came to an end as she felt mentally exhausted. However, she convinced herself that she would be far less stressed on her second day. Her group of children had been very well behaved and dearly hoped that would continue.

The second day was a more calm process as they had a relaxed morning with Jess as she'd found just how well their reading ability was. The afternoon would then be with Anne Wicks for their maths lesson. Jess actually sat in on this lesson, with Anne's agreement, to judge how well they were all dealing and coping with the maths questions, also to keep a motherly eye on young Tommy who Jess felt perhaps something was not quite right for him at home.

.

Chapter 10

Over the subsequent weeks Jess really enjoyed her work and had got to know all of the children, not only their names but to know them individually too. She managed to identify those who required special attention and the ones more than happy to get on with the task.

They'd had a few short history lessons together but Jess was determined for the children to learn and understand about pollution and climate change. As Jess had got to know the children very well and they, at the same time, had become more comfortable with her, she decided the next lesson would be the time to talk to them on this subject.

Jess, for some time, had felt so very strongly about what is happening to our planet. These children, and others like them, are the future and it will be their responsibility to help save planet Earth. As a brief lesson beforehand she proposed the following day's lesson would be about the planets and the solar system.

However, her class of children had lessons intermittently by Jane Phipps for English and Anne Wicks for Maths. Jess chose to sit in with these lessons if she so wished but on occasion would move to the Staff Room to prepare her own lesson. This she did in preparation to explain as simply as possible the planets and later climate change. With great thought about how to enthuse her class with this lesson, Jess needed to work out how to retain their interest which did require a little planning beforehand.

Later that day, on playground duty, Jess observed two boys from her class. Jack appeared to have pushed and shoved Bobby around who is a lot smaller and his behaviour was rather bossy. Jess did not intervene but continued to watch them surreptitiously.

Back in the classroom Jess reminded Jack about the story she had read to them on her first day. 'Do you remember the story about the Elephant and the Ant did you not learn anything Jack?' 'Yes Miss', he replied timidly. 'What were you doing to

Bobby in the playground then Jack?' who turned a shade of pink unaware that his teacher had watched him while on playground duty. 'Yes, I'm sorry Miss, I forgot'. 'Right, Jack that's good that you have apologised but now I would like you to apologise to Bobby'. Jack turned to Bobby and said 'sorry'.

So children let that be a lesson for everyone to be kind to one another, as in the story I read to you about the Elephant and the Ant. Jess then continued with her lesson.

'Our lesson today is going to be about the planets'. At the same time Jess handed a diagram to each child, which she'd painstakingly drawn and copied to, hopefully, help them as much as possible. Jess had drawn a plan of each planet on the board also.

'I would like you to copy down in your exercise book each planet as I have drawn and to write down the name of each individual one as I have done'. 'If any of you are struggling, please let me know and I will come and help. The diagram will help you too'.

Jess had drawn a huge yellow circle for the Sun then added the planets in the order they are in our solar system. Whilst the children are busy drawing the planets, Jess explained to her pupils that our Sun is a huge ball of Fire. It is millions of miles away and keeps us warm. When we have hot summer days though, we must use sun cream to prevent our bodies from going red or perhaps blistering from the heat of the sun.

'You will see there are 8 planets; I have named them in the order of our solar system'. 'We have Mercury, Venus, Earth, Mars, Jupiter, Saturn, Uranus and Neptune. 'Now remember to write the name across each planet as I have done so that you will all know which planet is which'.

Jess then went through each individual planet as she had drawn on the Board which gave the children time to write the name across the middle of each one. 'You will see that Jupiter and Saturn are the largest planets in our solar system and the solar system is called The Milky Way'.

Jess checked that they all have had time to write down the names but noticed that Tommy appeared to be having difficulty. Jess walked over to his desk to give him a hand as she can see he has done very little.

'Did you enjoy learning about the planets Tommy?' questioned Jess. 'I don't know' Tommy replied. 'What did you find difficult' asked Jess. 'I was tired and couldn't keep up' he very quietly responded. 'Why are you so tired'. 'I don't know' said Tommy. Jess a little concerned sat beside him at his desk and finished the drawings and wrote down the names of the planets for him. Quietly she said 'now do you think you could try to learn the names of the planets and the order they are from the Sun'. 'Yes, Miss, he replied.

As she turned to the rest of her class, Jess reiterated try and learn the names of the planets and the order they are in from the Sun. She told them that she would check later to find out what they had learned before their lesson about our own planet Earth one day soon.

'Do you have any questions for me before we finish this lesson?' Jess asked her class. David waved his hand in the air for a question, 'yes David'. 'Which planet is nearest to the sun, Miss?' 'David had you been listening I did explain how far away each planet was from the sun. I will repeat this, it is Mercury. 'If you look at the diagram I handed out to you all before our lesson started, you will see the nearest planet to the sun and the names of the planets next to Mercury and so on until you see that Neptune is the furthest away.

Becky then asked a question 'Which other planet can we live on?' Jess replied 'After Earth, Mars is the most habitable planet in our solar system due to several reasons: Its soil contains water to extract. It isn't too cold or too hot and there is enough sunlight to use solar panels. However you cannot breathe on Mars without a pressure suit as Mars has 96% carbon dioxide and only 0.1% oxygen. Earth has 21% oxygen'.

The children appeared satisfied so Jess dismissed the class and reminded them to study and learn about the lesson they'd had that day.

In the Staff Room later Jane asked Jess how she was getting along with all of her pupils. Jess replied that she believed she had a lovely and enthusiastic bunch of children and had got to know them all pretty well. Also she'd eventually worked them out to understand and learn about them as individuals.

However, Jess reported that she continued to be a little worried about Tommy. Jess had met Jane a number of times and had learned that she taught these same children when they were a younger. 'When Tommy was in my English class a couple of years ago, I perceived him to be a bright young boy with good manners and a joy to teach. I'm not sure what might have happened to him but, by what you say, he seemed to have changed remarkably' Jane commented. Jess was rather concerned to hear that and felt she really must continue to do her best to keep a special eye on him in the future.

A few days later Jess had tested the children on their lesson about the planets and was very impressed and happy to hear what most of them had absorbed. Clearly, they'd enjoyed the lesson very much.

It was now the last day of term so Jess decided to have a little learning game with the children. She believed that they had worked extremely hard for their new teacher and the time was right for them to have a little fun.

'Children we're going to have a little interactivity together so, first of all, I would like you to get into two teams. The children on the left hand side of the classroom will be one team and the children on the right the other team'. Richard's hand shot up 'but Miss they will have an extra person on their team'. Jess immediately thought that rather astute of him as there are 25 children in her class. 'Ok, Richard I do know that but you will see I have a chair in the front to face you all. We will call that chair 'the hot seat' and I will choose a child to sit in that seat then you will have the same number in each team'. Jess can see from Richard's expression that he thought that was now fair. Also Jess must very quickly choose a child to take the hot seat and thought Hannah, who is one of the brightest girls, should be in the hot seat first.

'Hannah, would you come and take the hot seat in front please'. Hannah walked to the front of the class to take the seat. Jess then explained to the children that she was going to draw a picture on the board and Hannah must try to guess what the picture is without looking. 'So children let's have a little practice first'. Jess started to draw the Sun on the Board. 'In your little groups talk quietly together and choose someone to stand up to say something to Hannah about the picture without telling her exactly the name. For instance 'is it hot'. 'So you see what I mean try to mislead Hannah but you must say the truth, but you don't want Hannah to guess straight away, do you all understand?' 'Yes' they all chime.

The next picture Jess drew was planet Earth. The children seemed to have great fun first one team said 'it's round', the next team 'there's a lot of water' and so on. They were all very good and did not want Hannah to know immediately but she soon guessed and the hot seat was changed for another pupil. 'Who would like to be in the hot seat next' questioned Jess. Several hands waved in the air so this time Jess chose a boy, Alex. Hannah then returned to Alex's seat.

Jess can see this interactive game gave the children a lot of joy and pleasure. They became very good at misleading the child in the hot seat by discussing quietly together in their teams how to do this honestly. Jess is very impressed with them. The hot seat changed several times so most of the children got an opportunity to guess the picture displayed on the board. A pretty little girl waved her hand to ask a question 'Yes Pippa' 'Can we do it again Miss'. 'I'm sure we can another day' said Jess. 'I shall look forward to seeing you all after half term' and with a cheery wave dismissed her class for their maths lesson.

However, Tommy does not appear to be so enthusiastic about leaving and looked rather downcast. 'What's the matter Tommy' asked Jess. 'I want my Mummy to be alright but she's not very well' he said. Jess took hold of both his hands in hers and said 'try to remember that your Mummy will need your help if she is sick. Be a big boy for me and see if you can be helpful for Mummy, will you try? 'Yes, Miss' he agreed. Jess continued 'I will look forward to seeing you after half term when you can then tell me how Mummy is, ok'. Tommy nodded and off he trotted and looked a wee happier.

Jess really felt that she would like to take him to his home, see his parents and find out exactly how sick his mother is and if his father is coping. However, as a teacher that could be seen as being rather intrusive. She must remember to question Tommy after half term to check how he is feeling.

Jess went home rather exhausted but happy with the progress her class seemed to have made. However, she was terribly worried about little Tommy and wanted to help him in any way possible but 'how' was the thought that mulled through her head.

Chapter 11

On Friday, before the start of half term, Jess contacted her mother after school as she felt she really should make a trip home to see her parents and sister. Although she'd kept in regular contact with her mother Jess had been far too busy to visit for some while and so arranged to go for Sunday lunch.

Her mother, Grace, a Music Teacher gave piano lessons to youngsters in her spare time. Jess did, however, take piano lessons from her mother and used to enjoy playing from time to time but now had other far more demanding pressures. Her father, a medical scientist, always did his best to help health professionals evaluate, diagnose and treat illnesses in the best way possible.

Jess is most proud of her father who, at one time, did his utmost to encourage her into this type of occupation, but it did not appeal to her one iota.

Her younger sister, Holly, completely different to Jess, is extremely musical with a beautiful soprano voice.

Jess took the long bus ride to her parents, as she walked through the door 'hello Mum' and gave each other a most welcome hug. Grace overjoyed to see her eldest daughter at long last. Dad, Ted, and Holly heard the commotion and came quickly to greet her.

With so much to catch up and talk about they all seemed to ask questions at the same time. 'Ok' said her mother 'let us listen and hear what Jess has to say first'. Jess as quickly as possible enlightened them about her school and the children. Also enlarged on the holiday she'd taken to Hawaii with her college best friend Josie, although they had briefly spoken about it over the telephone. All goggled eyed as they listened to Jess, her mother left them to continue as she quietly went to the kitchen.

Now sitting at the dining table together, Grace brought in their already plated Sunday lunch of roast lamb, potatoes and veg, together with the accompanying mint sauce. 'This looks yummy Mum, thank you' Jess retorted as she tucked in.

Holly with her beautiful golden hair and pretty smile is a smart, kind, funny and overall amazing girl. 'I haven't really mentioned this to you over the telephone' said Holly 'but Mum was asked to play the piano at a concert and needed someone to sing a song half way through her performance, so she asked me. I was very reluctant, of course, but agreed. I was noticed by someone desperate for a soprano to sing in a forthcoming show. Can you believe that?' 'Wow' Jess remarked 'How wonderful'.

Holly continued 'I've been asked to possibly sing in a show in a few months' time. I'm not too sure what it is at the moment but I believe it may be Les Mis, a musical which I would love. I had actually picked up snippets that I may be asked to sing 'On My Own' that is if it is decided this is the show they should go for. The Director will let me know for sure in due course and to confirm whether or not I'm still wanted. My guess is they may well be searching for other sopranos, who knows?

'Oh my goodness, that would be wonderful, I'm sure you will be chosen' Jess retorted 'do let me know as soon as you hear won't you?' said Jess. 'Of course I will' exclaimed Holly. 'I believe rehearsals must start fairly soon so I'm sure I won't be kept waiting much longer to know one way or another'.

'So I'm probably going to have a famous sister' said an excited Jess. 'Oh don't be silly' said Holly 'I'm pretty sure it will be a fairly small part anyway'. 'So what about your job' Jess continued. 'I've spoken to my boss and I'm going to be allowed time off to attend rehearsals if required'.

Holly is an Accountant for a small firm who rely on her implicitly. Her firm would, of course, do everything in their power to keep her as she is totally relied upon.

'We're very proud of her' expressed Grace. 'Yes, I'm sure you are Mum' Jess replied 'as I am too. Well done Holly, I do hope you accept if offered this wonderful opportunity. I shall look forward to the day when I can see you perform, fingers crossed'.

'How's the new boyfriend, Chris, you met a few weeks ago?' Jess enquired. 'Well we've met up a couple of times but early days yet' said Holly. Jess with a slight glance towards her mother had a strange feeling somehow her parents did not approve but perhaps she imagined it.

All this catch-up they'd managed before a delightful pudding is brought in, which is Jess's favourite, Pavlova with Raspberry sauce.

'Gosh Mum, that was absolutely delicious, thank you so much'. Jess helped her mother with the dishes before she departed. With lots of hugs they all said a cheery goodbye and her father walked her to the nearby bus stop. Jess refused to allow him to take her back in his car as she had a return bus ticket anyway and the journey wasn't that long. It was, of course, half term so she had time on her side.

On the return journey Jess's thoughts meandered around her successful family and how proud she was of them all. However, she realised that not everyone would have been as lucky brought up in a loving and positive way. This made her think of little Tommy again and what he must be going through at this time with his mother so very sick.

Jess pondered over the look her mother gave her when Holly's boyfriend was mentioned. She had a quiet word with her mother about him before she left. 'I'm not sure what it is Jess but he has looked rather vacant the few times I've met him and I wondered if he had mood swings. I'm concerned for Holly but she does appear to be rather fond of him'. 'Oh maybe you've imagined it Mum, Holly is so smart I cannot envisage her being so friendly with a feeble or wayward character'. 'Yes, perhaps you're right I must try not to be too protective of her'.

Jess was so pleased that she'd made the effort to visit her parents and to enable her to catch up with Holly too.

Chapter 12

Mike, whom Jess had met briefly over dinner after being introduced by her friend Josie, together with another of her friends Jeff, telephoned early the next day after supper. Josie had intimated that Mike really liked her and wondered if he might invite her out sometime. Jess saw him as attractive and friendly but nothing more and had pushed him out of her mind so much so she was, in fact, wholly surprised to hear his voice at the other end of the telephone, especially after so long after the four of them had had dinner together.

'Hello' said Jess in answer to the telephone ring 'Hello Jess, Mike here, do you remember when we met for dinner with Josie and Jeff should you have forgotten'. 'Hello Mike, yes I do remember, Jess replied. 'Oh that's good' he responded 'I appreciate it's been rather a long while since then. I wouldn't have been in the least surprised if it had slipped your mind completely. 'Anyway I wondered if you'd like to meet up for coffee, in a day or so, I've heard how extremely busy you've been?' After his lengthy explanation Jess thought quickly then responded with a 'yes that would be nice'. 'I don't suppose you can make this Saturday, as I'm free and hope you may well be too, if you'd like to of course'. Jess thought again for a brief moment, with the thought that she had a lot of class-work to prepare but answered 'yes, why not, it would be good to see you and also get me away for a short while from my paper work'.

Josie had talked somewhat to Jess about Jeff and Mike when they were on holiday together, as their work schedules would periodically keep them in close touch. This had helped Jess not to forget Mike completely, although he was never in the forefront of her mind at any one time. After their brief chat they arranged to meet outside the local Coffee Bar at 11am on Saturday.

The day soon arrived and with just a short distance away from where she lived, Jess walked to the Coffee Bar and saw Mike as he waited outside. 'Hello nice to see you again' and took her hand in his rather formally. 'Hello' said Jess as they walked into the Coffee Bar.

Sat down with their coffee, he asked if Jess would like a snack but she kindly refused with a thank you. Mike looked intently at her as he spoke 'I didn't contact you before now as I said I'd heard from Josie that you were very busy with your school work which, I imagine, you must have a lot of preparation to do one way and another. I presumed it best for you to get settled into your new job first, although I really would have liked to ask you out sooner'.

Mike told her this little story as he didn't wish her to know his real reason for not making contact before now.

On the other hand to Jess that seemed a poor excuse as she was now many months into her, supposedly, new job. However she responded with 'oh that was really sweet and thoughtful of you'.

'So tell me exactly what you do Mike' requested Jess. 'I can't really tell you much except that I work as a Crime Investigator or Specialist Investigator for complex cases.

I've done this job now for a few years' Mike retorted. Jess had realised that some of his work may be secret, or rather not to be carelessly talked about so replied 'Oh that must be so interesting. I guess there are certain aspects of your work that you shouldn't relay to others'. 'Yes you're right'. However there are a few things I could mention but not share specific cases' he commented. 'Of course' replied a respectful Jess. Questions about his work gave Jess something to talk to him about as she was terribly unsure of him, whatever he indicated.

'I don't wish to bore you with my situation, I would rather like to get to know you a little better' Mike requested. 'Ok' said Jess and told him briefly about her job and the children she taught and also a little about the main subjects she'd been doing her level best to teach. Also how grateful she was to have a really nice bunch of pupils in her class.

Despite their conversation with each other about work, they appeared to enjoy one another's company as they got on reasonably well, although Jess sensed Mike to be a little uptight. However, she was very relaxed as they smiled and laughed at some silly incidences that they'd both experienced which they shared. Josie had obviously given him a little information about their trip to Hawaii which Mike brought into the conversation. Jess confirmed and enlightened him on a couple of joyous occasions which he appeared to thoroughly enjoy as he listened to her story.

Jess peered at her watch and felt the time was now right to draw their brief encounter to a close as she was sure Mike had much to do as well.

As they left the Coffee Bar, the sky is a blindingly bright blue, dotted here and there with fluffy white clouds as they scurried along on the gentle breeze. The boughs of the cherry trees weighed heavily beneath the cluster of ripening buds as they start to open.

Blackbirds were winging their way down into the garden, their little feet stamping the ground to persuade out the unsuspecting worms which were promptly snapped up into those long vivid yellow beaks.

What a wonderful day Jess thought before they departed from a very nice coffee session together. Mike took her hand into his and said 'would you mind if I keep in touch and perhaps arrange for us to meet up again sometime when we're both free? 'Yes, I would really like that and thank you so much for the coffee and delightful company' said Jess. Mike squeezed her hand and gently pecked her on both cheeks before they said their farewells. Jess was happy in Mike's company, although she felt reticent as to his real opinion of her but still hoped he would call again before too long.

As they turned and walked in opposite directions both, simultaneously, looked back and waved. Jess on cloud nine, despite her doubt, as Mike was so pleasant and comfortable to be with. It had been some time since Jess had had the company of a really nice male companion, who helped her feel wonderfully relaxed and happy.

Jess, of course, would not know the thoughts that soared through Mike's mind at the time. He truly felt that he was forcing himself to be nice, friendly and chatty towards Jess, almost like an act. Although there was nothing to dislike about her, in fact he rather liked her friendliness and intelligence and attractiveness too. But always at the back of his mind was this nagging disloyalty towards Lucy, the wonderful girlfriend he'd lost. On the other hand his good pal Jeff continued, as always, to encourage him to at least try to get on with his life

From a distance Jess spotted Claire outside the house watering the few plants in her front garden. Jess had mentioned that she was to meet Mike for coffee so as she approached home, Claire greeted her and, of course, wished to know how they'd got on.

'Oh come on in for a cup of tea Claire when you've finished, we can have a little chat'. 'OK, thanks' said Claire and immediately placed her watering can onto the ground and followed her inside.

'So how did it go?' said Claire who cannot wait to hear what Jess had to say about her brief meet up with Mike. 'Well, he's really nice, very caring and sympathetic, I liked him very much. He mentioned the holiday Josie and I had when we went to Hawaii and the wonderful couple Bruce and Harriet we ended up with who took pity and cared for us for three days. He appeared very interested to know what could have turned out to be a very traumatic time for us but was, in fact, blessed in the end. That to me showed his caring side'. Jess continued with 'he said very little about his job, was interested to hear about mine though.

So, maybe next time we'll find out a little more about each other'. 'Oh, so there's going to be a next time then?' 'Yes, hopefully, he said he would call again and perhaps we could meet up when we're both free' she said to Claire with her enquiring mind.

'What about you Claire, anyone you're interested in on the horizon?' Jess asked. 'No, not really' 'but there is a doctor at the hospital I could be most interested in but I don't think he's noticed me in that way, although our paths have crossed several times. 'I do know he's not married and guess he's a few years older than me but no idea if he has a girlfriend. It's very difficult to have a personal conversation with him. He's always so very busy with patients'. 'Oh that's sad, Jess remarked 'I hope he's noticed you as a lovely and attractive girl rather than an efficient co-worker'. 'Fingers crossed' replied Claire.

Chapter 13

Now back to the class room after half term, Jess believed the children are now ready to learn a little more about our planet Earth.

Welcomed the children into class after the short half term holiday and hoped they'd had an enjoyable few days away from school. Now all seated explained 'we have already learned about the planets in our solar system and now I believe you should all try and know a little more about our own. So, this morning we're going to talk about our planet Earth.

'I would like you to make notes in your exercise books. Then when we return to school after the long summer holiday, we will have a memory lesson to see what you all remember. I have made some notes on the board to help you so copy them down in your exercise books and read them occasionally. This will help you learn from your own words'.

Jess continued: 'Earth is the 3rd planet from the Sun after Mercury and Venus. Earth is where we live and looks blue from space because it is mainly covered by water. Earth is the 5th largest planet in the solar system but all the planets are tiny compared with the Sun. It takes 365 days for Earth to revolve around the Sun and the Moon takes 24 hours to revolve around the Earth. The Moon we see from Earth is the light from the Sun. The gravity of the Sun pulls the planets towards it. No living thing can survive without the Sun'. Jess thought she'd mentioned Earth too many times but reminded herself that she is teaching and talking to 8 and 9 year old children.

A hand shot up for a question 'Yes Ruby' asked Jess. 'Why doesn't the Sun pull all the planets into it?' 'That's a very good question Ruby. It's because each planet is moving at great speed around the Sun, so it is impossible for the Sun to pull in the planets'. Jess carried on.

'Mercury is the closest planet to the Sun, but it is Venus that is the hottest planet in the solar system'.

Another hand shot up for a question 'Yes, Bobby'. 'Why is Venus the hottest planet when Mercury is closest to the Sun?'

'Well that's an excellent question too Bobby. This is because Mercury doesn't have any atmosphere and atmosphere can trap and hold heat. This thick atmosphere will make the surface of Venus hotter because the heat doesn't escape back into space'.

A hand is raised for another question when Richard asked 'what is atmosphere, Miss?' 'Atmosphere Richard is a thick envelope of air around the earth which is called atmosphere. Air is a mixture of many gases like oxygen, nitrogen, carbon dioxide etc. We inhale oxygen from the air and breathe out carbon dioxide.

Now we all have the planets and their names in our exercise books, I would like you to learn them and next time we'll discuss them a little more. However, over the next few weeks I would like you to study your drawings from your exercise books and try to learn what we have talked about today by studying the pictures and the names of the planets. Next time we will discuss more about our Earth, what we are doing and have done over the years and how it is affecting how our climate is changing.

This afternoon we will have a nice quiet time and read a story together'. The school bell then rang for their lunch break, but the children did not move until Jess said they could go which she thought extremely polite and good mannered of them, as always.

'Tommy, would you bring your exercise book to me before you go'. So Tommy did as he was told and brought his book over to Jess who could see very little had been written in his book on their lesson.

'Did you enjoy what we learned about the planets this morning?' 'Mmmmmm' was little Tommy's weak reply. 'How is Mummy?' 'She's still not very well' said the sad small boy. Jess continued 'whenever you feel sad, will you please come to me and we can have a chat together to help you feel a little better'.

Jess quickly wrote a few major points down for him in his book. 'Now Tommy over the next school holiday do you think you could try and learn some of the things I have written down for you in your book?' 'Yes, Miss', Tommy seemed to whisper. 'Good boy' said Jess 'I would like you to know as much as the other children in class when I question you all next term'. Tommy nodded and took his book back to his desk then skipped off.

Chapter 14

The children returned after their lunch break when Jess relayed to them. 'Well after our difficult lesson this morning about our planet Earth, do you think it would be nice for you to have a story this afternoon? 'Yes, please Miss', most of her class chanted. 'Right then, here we go.

This is a story about a 12 year old girl whose father had died the year before and she had been very heartbroken. The young girl was now beginning to understand that her father was gone and would never return. Her mother was at work and she was left alone during the school Easter holiday. So this is her story.'

As it was the Easter school holiday, Jill said to her friend Mary 'let's go for a bike-ride'. 'Ok' agreed Mary, 'we've nothing much else to do today'. Mary was a year older than Jill, and they weren't even attending the same school. However, they lived near to each other and had become firm friends.

So off they went together not knowing quite where they were going, but headed off from Oxford onto the long and winding London Road. They had such fun on their journey with very few cars on the roads then. There were many twists and turns in the road when they took their feet off the pedals and shouted happily together as they whizzed down the hills.

As they cycled along they saw a recreation ground 'shall we stop here for a swing' yelled Jill. 'Yes' bellowed Mary. 'We could do with a rest then perhaps we should start to think about turning back' she said. They had the swings to themselves and had great fun as both girls tried to see how high they could go. Now time to leave. 'Shall we go a little further' said Jill, encouraging Mary to agree 'Alright' answered Mary 'but it will get dark quite early'.

Darkness, of course, came rather early at that time of year, which somehow must have completely slipped their minds as they were having so much fun. However they had failed to realise just how much further away from home they now were.

The light was beginning to fade and they had no lamps on their bicycles. The girls hopped off their bicycles for a little break in a quiet spot and discussed together what they should do next. Mary seemed more concerned than Jill, and said 'We have to ride back so we'd better go quickly before it gets too dark'. 'Yes we must' Jill agreed. As they turned their bicycles around to head back a policeman approached. He was nice and friendly and in a calm manner asked 'what are you doing here?' 'We just came for a bike-ride' they both chanted. The policeman proceeded with 'where have you come from?' 'Oxford' they replied in unison. 'Oxford', he almost screeched 'I think you'd better come along with me'.

The policeman could see they were two young girls who would never have made it back home to Oxford before dark.

So off they trotted with their bicycles alongside the policeman. He took them to his local police station, where they were warmly greeted and given tea and a sandwich, which they thoroughly enjoyed as both were starving hungry by this time. It was now early evening and getting very dark and the girls began to wonder how on earth they were going to get back home. At this point they suddenly heard a very loud voice which came from a policewoman, both girls heard her as she yelled 'brats and kids, what have they been up to?' Jill and Mary were now terribly frightened when they heard this remark, especially when the police woman approached them and started to ask questions in a very hostile manner. She then swiftly turned and disappeared.

The other policemen at the station didn't say very much but continued to be friendly towards them. They were now too terrified to ask how they were going to get home, so remained quiet.

The hostile policewoman returned some time later. Firstly, she turned to Mary 'I have been in touch with your parents who were both at home' she remarked coldly, then turned to face Jill 'as for you, your mother is at a dance'. Jill felt so embarrassed, and her face turned bright red as she felt very guilty about her mother.

It had become rather late when eventually the policewoman said, 'you two come with me'. Both girls were too afraid to question where they were going. Told to get into a police car, completely unaware of where they were being taken. Eventually, the car stopped outside a very large house and were told 'come along', so they got out of the car and were taken into, what turned out to be a children's home, where both were then told they would stay the night. A lovely homely lady greeted them and put her finger to her lips to show them to be quiet and to remove their shoes. They then quietly ascended the stairs and were taken to a dormitory.

They were each shown a bed and left to sleep. When alone, both girls looked at the sleeping children in the rows of beds when Jill said 'We'll make their beds for them in the morning'. Mary said 'I need the toilet'. The matron, however, hadn't told them where the toilets were, so they quietly crept around to try to find them. Unfortunately, they couldn't find any so, as they both needed to use the toilet before getting into bed, found a row of sinks which were quite low and had to use them instead. [Jess heard some of the children as they giggled at this statement but Jess ignored it and continued].

The following morning they awoke from a much-needed sleep and saw that all of the other beds were empty. The children the girls had seen asleep when they arrived, must have been extremely quiet, as Jill and Mary had not heard a sound. The girls quickly dressed and went down the stairs and followed the excited chatter of children, who they found sitting around a long table having breakfast together.

They were not all little children, as both girls had imagined, and some were about their age. The matron welcomed them with a 'good morning girls' then showed them to a seat at the table and with a smile on her face said 'tuck in and have some breakfast'. 'Thank you' replied Jill and Mary and sat down with the other children. Some of the older girls were very interested, asked what they were doing there so, between mouthfuls, as they were both extremely hungry, they talked about their bicycle ride from Oxford and explained how they had gone a little too far. The children became very absorbed with their tale. After breakfast, all of the children were ushered into the garden.

Jill and Mary continued to chat away with the other children, now having a very happy time, with no thought of home. It was entertaining and most enjoyable to talk with some of the girls, who were so friendly and appeared to be very happy in the home.

Later, milk and biscuits were brought out and given to everyone in the garden as the weather was nice but a little cool, but none of them seemed to feel the slight chill in the air.

Suddenly, one of the girls, Lisa, saw the policewoman arrive. Jill and Mary had told Lisa that she had been rather cross and not very nice to them. The policewoman had a bunch of flowers in her hand, and Lisa exclaimed jokingly, 'she's come to put you in your boxes'. Lisa giggled whilst saying this.

'You two come with me,' the policewoman beckoned, so Jill and Mary said a quick goodbye to Lisa and the others and followed the policewoman. 'Your bicycles are going to be returned to Oxford on the train', she explained. 'I'm now going to take you both to the coach station, where the coach will take you home', she continued. So, like little lambs the girls followed her to her car and climbed in without a word. They were given a small packed lunch for their journey. Sheepishly they said goodbye to the policewoman and boarded the coach, where they sat together on the back seat. They tucked into their food immediately, when Mary retorted 'this is fun!' Jill agreed as she couldn't remember when she had last enjoyed herself so much, albeit very scary at times.

The girls had been on the coach for what, to them, seemed rather a long while when they noticed the coach was approaching near to where they lived. Mary said to Jill 'Go and ask the driver if he would drop us off at the next roundabout!' Jill walked to the front of the coach and asked the driver 'Would you please drop us off at the next roundabout? 'Get back to your seat', cried the driver in a cross manner. Jill returned to her seat and said to Mary 'He won't let us off'.

Three miles further on, the coach arrived at the terminus, when the other passengers left the coach. The driver then locked the door with Mary and Jill still quietly sitting on the back seat. Before he did so, he glanced at them but didn't say a word. Eventually, he came back, unlocked the door and beckoned to them. They were taken into an office, when the other drivers there asked 'so what have you young ladies been up to?' 'We just went for a bike ride' explained Jill 'and went too far'. After Jill's explanation, their driver was a lot kinder and said 'we thought you'd been naughty girls'. The girls were then told that they had to wait for one of their parents to collect them before they would be allowed home.

A short while later, Jill's mother sauntered into the bus station, looked very smart and smiled, not scolding them at all. She had a few words with some of the drivers and then escorted both girls home.*[1]

'So you see boys and girls do not ever go too far away from home', Jess warned.

'That's the end of the story children, I hope you liked it'. Hands then start to wave in the air to ask Jess questions which she did her best to answer. There is no need to ask them questions as she'd intended as they'd obviously listened absorbed with interest, even little Tommy whom she'd helped from time to time. Jess was really pleased that she'd been able to hold the children's attention with the story. In fact she believed they loved it.

Chapter 15

In the staff room later Jess mentioned Tommy again to Jane about him falling asleep in class as she'd taught Tommy when he was younger. Jane believed he became troubled by his mother's illness.

Jane had enquired some while ago when she'd heard his mother was very sick, which of course by now Jess was aware. His mother's illness was exceedingly difficult for him and seemed to have completely changed little Tommy.

'Life must be a struggle at home with his mother so sick, his father must be finding it most difficult to care for Tommy and his sister who is a little older' said Jane.

'I can understand why he's shown little interest in school work and does tend to fall asleep in class Jess replied. 'I really would like to take him under my wing and do my level best to help him. However the only way I believe I can do that would be by doing my best to keep him as often as possible for a short while after lessons. Principally to take a special interest in him and help wherever I can'. 'Yes, I believe that would be a good start to see if it might help' confirmed Jane.

Jess started to give Tommy a little special attention. He stayed after class one day and opened up to her about his Mummy. Jess's heart felt near breaking point as she listened to this sorrowful wee lad as he talked about his Mummy. She wanted to engulf him in her arms to protect and care for him and repeated, as Jess had, of course, mentioned this to him before. 'If you are sad and worried I would like you to come to me after lessons and perhaps we can have a wee chat together to see if it will make you feel a little better, is that ok'. 'Yes' said Tommy and off he went with a look not quite so very sad.

After the children have had their Maths and English lessons with other teachers, Jess with her class again ready to teach more general studies.

In the meantime and before the end of term, Jess had worked at her school for some long while when Head teacher, Miss Orchard, approached her whilst in the staff room as she took a well needed short break. 'Jess I have been aware for some time just how much you have become involved in climate change.

We have a Teacher's Conference coming up in the not too distant future. I've been asked if anyone in my school would like to take part, either in a discussion group or to give a lecture on a subject of interest. How would you feel if I asked, or rather, persuaded you to take part?' Dora Orchard asked.

Jess pondered for a short moment. 'Yes, I would rather like that' she replied and continued. 'However, I would definitely require time to put a paper together. As you know I have been involved with climate change for some time now and this topic is what I'd feel most strongly to talk about'.

'Well you don't have to make a decision immediately' Dora Orchard responded. 'I suggest you take a couple of days to mull it over, and get back to me'. 'Thank you' Jess replied. 'I do need to consider a number of points, whether I am indeed capable of speaking to a vast audience in a positive and interesting way about my passion. Also time to work on details of importance and concern to, hopefully, capture their interest and its significance'.

'Marvellous' responded Dora Orchard. 'Well the Conference will be at the end of September which should, I imagine, give you enough time if in a day or two for you decide positively to go ahead and are able to put your thoughts together to take on this challenge?' 'I hope I can' said Jess. 'I will most seriously think this through over the next couple of days and get back to you. If I do feel I have the courage to take on this task I will, of course, do my level best to get everything together in time'.

As she left the staff room for her class. Jess wondered what on earth had she almost agreed to do and sincerely hoped she could possibly be ready for this challenging assignment. Also she did realise it would be a lot of extra work for her in preparation. However, it would be a way of getting over to people her passion on global warming and climate change. Should she or should she not do it? This an almighty decision for her to make.

Jess pulled herself together for her next lesson but Miss Orchard's conference request remained deep in her mind.

Chapter 16

The children had absorbed and enjoyed their lesson on the planets and also on our planet Earth and Jess is sure they should now be ready for a lesson about the Ozone Layer, Greenhouse gas and Pollution. However she must keep it as simple as possible to ensure it's not too difficult for them to understand.

'Right children' Jess greeted them brightly 'we're going to talk about the ozone layer, greenhouse gas and pollution this morning'.

Some of the children looked ready and happy to listen to this sequence of events. Others she was not too sure about so Jess, again, reminded herself to make it as interesting and as uncomplicated as she can.

Here we go she thought. 'The ozone layer surrounds Earth, it is our protective shield. This keeps us safe from the harmful rays of the sun which absorbs most of the ultraviolet radiation.

When pollution makes holes in the ozone layer, more of this ultraviolet radiation can reach the surface of the earth - which can cause potential harm to humans and other living things.

Ultraviolet rays can damage DNA and cause sunburn, increasing the long-term risk of problems such as skin cancer. DNA is Deoxyribonucleic Acid which is like a recipe book which holds the instructions for making all the proteins in our bodies. DNA is what makes you, you.

Greenhouse gases make holes in the ozone layer which allows more heat to reach Earth. This prevents heat from escaping into space, therefore warming our planet. Too much greenhouse gas will make Earth too hot but without greenhouse gases Earth would be an icy wasteland. So you see children we need a balance. As I said too much pollution will make our planet too hot'.

About 30 years ago scientists found that there were holes beginning to appear in the ozone layer. These holes were being caused by various substances used by us humans like fossil fuels the main reason we have pollution. The ozone holes do not cause global warming but affects atmospheric circulation which is the movement of air and the ocean circulation. The ocean current is dominated by a number of forces acting upon the water, like the Earth's rotation, wind and temperature. This allows thermal energy (heat) to be redistributed onto the surface of the Earth'.

Whilst she spoke to her class Jess began to set up a video of illustrations and pictures to enable the children to better understand what might appear a little complicated.

Jess continued with the hope that the children would not be bored but interested enough to follow what she had to show in detailed pictures, together with her words.

'We will now have a very brief chat about pollution and how, if we use, less harmful substances the holes will begin to disappear in the ozone layer.

The main cause of pollution is the burning of fossil fuels, such as coal, oil and gas. Waste in landfills, where all of our rubbish is buried, together with the exhausts from all vehicles and a whole lot of other human activities which are known as Earth's pollution'. Jess then brought up pictures of various waste deposits, the source of pollution.

'You may wonder where did fossil fuels come from well I will explain a little about the history. Fossil fuels formed in the Earth hundreds of millions of years ago when Earth had huge tropical forests. During those periods plants and animals lived, grew, and died. As these plants and animals decomposed their remains sank into the mud and rock. Those remains would undergo chemical and physical changes and eventually became fossil fuels. Over millions of years many layers of rock would build up and the remains of plants and animals slowly changed and also became fossil fuels.

Coal was formed from dead trees and other plant material. Coal miners during the 19th century were then able to dig up this solid fuel to be used all over the world.

Plankton, on the other hand, are small microscopic organisms that died and fell to the bottom of the sea. Over millions of years the plankton became trapped under many layers of sand and mud. The heat and pressure from rocks would gradually build up also undergo chemical and physical changes which over millions of years turned into natural gas and oil.

Plankton decomposed into natural gas and oil, while plants became coal.

'I'm going to hand out a poem to each of you about the Sun, the Earth and Pollution which will help you to make more sense of what is actually happening to our planet. I hope you will read and enjoy the poem'. Jess explained this as she handed a copy to each child.

My Planet was quite beautiful once upon a time
And now I have these carbons which will ruin my fine line
My mate the sun we got on well before we had this dust
Now we have this murk and dust coming right between us
I wish those humans down below would stop what they are doing
Their chimney smoke, exhausts from cars
Spewing! Spewing! Spewing!
I will still be here in a hundred years or more
But if they do not change their ways, they'll be splattered on the floor.
I've always liked to help in any way I can
But the time has come for them to take control and ban
Old habits and to change before it is too late
'Coz we can see where they are going me and my 'ole mate.
So start using those Renewables – Wind and Solar too
My mate the sun will help in any way that's true
Stop throwing all those carbons and change your ways my man
Because my friends I will be lonely here in space without the human race.[1]

'Children you will see that there is a space at the bottom of the page. I would like you all to copy the drawing from the board'.

The children could see that Jess had drawn a large circle which predicted the earth, with a rather glum face. She'd drawn clumps of pollution clouds as they surround the edge of the Earth which prevented the Sun, which Jess had drawn above the Earth, from penetrating its warmth.

'You may understand more clearly, from the drawing, the clouds of pollution which surround Earth. So children I hope you like the picture and the poem. It is the Earth trying to let us humans know what is happening and to help save our planet'.

Jess heard the school bell for their lunch break and hoped the children had done their best to understand the lesson. It was fairly obvious that they liked the poem and the drawing of the Earth as it looked so terribly unhappy surrounded by pollution.

Before Jess dismissed her class she reminded them that they hadn't quite completed their lesson on pollution and would continue the next day as they were due for their maths less with Anne Wicks.

'Good morning children we're going to complete our lesson today on pollution so

I'm going to start with car engines which burn fuel and then fumes come out of the exhaust which pollutes the air. That's why many car manufacturers are starting to build cars to use electricity instead of petrol and diesel.

Smoke is a type of pollution too. Many years ago people used coal and wood to keep warm which first started the pollution. At that time smog, which is a combination of fog and smoke, was a huge problem in the winter months as more coal was burnt to produce heat. In 1952 smog in London killed more than 4,000 people.

Jess could see the children appeared to seem quite interested. Obviously they'd heard from another source about climate change and how it would be the responsibility of young people to deal with this problem in the future.

Jess then explained how electricity is developed from Power Stations by burning fossil fuels such as coal and gas. Gases then go up the tall chimneys spewing out pollution into the air. 'So you see children how we must try to mend the holes in the ozone layer by having less pollution. This will save us from the harmful rays of the sun. You know on a very hot day in the summer if sun screen isn't used we will burn'.

Jess felt this was enough for them to absorb for the moment. At least they should now understand what the ozone layer is and how it is there to protect us.

She had noticed Tommy had fallen asleep, although the other children seemed to have enjoyed trying to understand her words. The children are dismissed for their lunch break and Jess gently awakens Tommy to join the others.

Jess found it rather difficult to sleep as she contemplated her decision to participate in the Conference. Is she up to it? Can she put into words the amount required to speak to many people gathered together in a huge Conference Room? All these points scurried through her brain. Yes, she must do this irrespective of her concern. This is her passion and a great opportunity to spread the word.

Once Jess had reached her decision to go ahead, she felt calmness within and began to relax once more.

Chapter 17

Claire popped in to see Jess when she arrived home from work with the knowledge that usually she was back from school before her.

Jess opened her door to the sound of the bell 'Hello Claire, come on in' she greeted. 'Thanks' said Claire and followed Jessica inside. Sat down together over a cup of tea, Claire looked hopefully at Jess 'I have two weeks off during July and I'm seriously thinking of taking a week's holiday to Ibiza and wondered if you would like to come with me?' 'Mm' Jess responded 'I guess it would be rather nice to get away for a week in the sun, let me think about it Claire and we'll have a chat over the weekend, is that ok with you'? 'Ok' answered Claire 'but you'll need to make a decision fairly quickly as I really want to make arrangements pretty soon'. 'Of course, it does sound a brilliant idea, I just need to get my head around my work schedule and get everything in order before I make a decision, so I'll let you know one way or the other by the weekend'. 'Great' said an excited Claire 'must leave you to it now as I feel you have a lot of school work to do'.

Now alone and while she looked through her children's class work books to mark, Jess meandered over Claire's proposition for a few days holiday to a sunny clime. Perhaps it would be a good idea and is rather drawn to have a break away. It was not long before the end of term, but Jess felt reasonably sure she could get everything in order to enable her to have a break away for a few days.

Also she had eventually become extremely despondent and rather disappointed with Mike as he hadn't been in touch, especially when he'd asked if she wouldn't mind if he kept in contact with her. This had helped reach a positive decision to go away for a few days. However, she again seriously mulled it over during the weekend to be absolutely confident and sure it was the right thing to do and, yes, she was definitely sure it would be really rather nice.

So eventually knocked on Claire's door, when she knew she should be home from work. Jess clarified her decision that she would very much like to get away and take the holiday to Ibiza with her. Claire was obviously ecstatic with Jess's decision. They then discussed and agreed the best week for them and Jess, with Claire's suggestion, left her to make the bookings as she'd already had some idea of the cost and the most suitable hotel for their stay with the research she'd managed to do earlier. It was agreed between them that they would go as soon as possible after the school holiday commenced; before the end of July when it would be less likely to have families everywhere with their excited and energetic children.

Jess began to look forward to this short break to Ibiza. During the final two weeks she enjoyed teaching her class of children before their long Summer Term holiday. She had not relayed to Dora Orchard her imminent trip to Ibiza, but thought she could use this period of peace and tranquillity to make notes for her participation at the upcoming Teachers' Conference. Jess felt this would ease the pressure on her to get her paper ready in time

Dora Orchard was excited and grateful when Jess approached her to confirm that she would in fact like to go ahead with writing a paper for the forthcoming Teachers Conference. Dora Orchard acknowledged Jess's judgement to do so and reiterated her proposal to help in any way possible.

Sadly, Jess learned at the same time that little Tommy's mother had passed away. Jess felt broken-hearted for him when she heard this and determined to help this little boy as much as she possibly could.

At the end of the school day Jess called Tommy over to her desk as the other children left the classroom. Jess had built a bond between her and this sad little boy and asked him if there was anything he'd like to talk to her about.

Tommy revealed just how sad he had been since his Mummy became very ill and then she left him. Obviously he meant his mother had passed away. Jess found it most difficult to keep the tears away from her eyes as this little boy felt confident enough to tell her, his teacher, just how he had been feeling.

Tommy looked down at his feet and stopped talking so Jess took both his hands in hers and said 'I'm going to tell you a little story and I would like you to think about it when you feel really sad and I hope it will make you less sad and maybe a little more happy'. He lifted his head and looked at Jess in wonder when she started to relay a story to him:

Someone very close has died
And now it hurts deep inside
It's not the same as feeling sad
None of my bumps ever hurt this bad
How did this happen, where did she go?
Is this something anyone can know
Why did this happen how can this be
That someone I love is no longer here with me
Wait, did I hear someone whispering
Is it possible something special is happening
What could this be?
Listen, what do I hear?
I can feel that you are near
Sleep dear Tommy you need your rest
When you wake you will feel refreshed
It will take time but you will see
I will show you ways to remember me
I am not gone just out of sight
Safe and happy and full of light
Now you'll feel my warm embrace
When the wind moves your hair and the sun kisses your face
Love endures even when you dream you'll find
That I will come and visit from time to time
It's ok to feel sad
That is when you should remember the fun we had
Tell our story to those we know
Your memories will make their hearts glow
Love our people and laugh with them too
They feel sad just like you
Now I need something from you my lovely child dear
It's the best way to keep me near
Remember the things I did best
That made you feel so loved and blessed

These are the things you can do too
Then through your actions I live on through you
All the joys that you gave me will always be cherished and dear to me
I had a wonderful life and you will too
If love is your guiding light
There's no need to worry, no need to hide
Whenever you need me, I'll be by your side
Someday we'll meet again until then remember my hugs and my warm embrace
And know that your love will always bring a smile to my face
This world is not our home we are just passing through
Someday we'll meet again
Until then, remember I LOVE YOU! *?

Tommy looked up at Jess with eyes that looked watery but he did not cry. With a wee smile upon his face he managed a wee 'thank you'. Jess, felt rather emotional herself kissed his hand, explained the word embrace to him and handed him the poem to take home in the hope that it would lift his spirit and help him in the days ahead.

'Try to remember Tommy, when you feel really sad, read this poem again and it will help you to smile through your sadness' said Jess, his two little hands still clasped in hers and gave them a squeeze before she let them go. 'Bye' and off he skipped with a brief smile upon his face as he clutched the poem tightly in his hand.

Jess truly hoped that it would be a turning point for Tommy. She had been able to find out from the school staff about his home life and that he did have a good father. However, for a boy so young not to have his loving Mummy any more, Jess can truly understand at times his depth of despair.

Chapter 18

It was Saturday morning when 'ping' the telephone rang which disturbed her train of thought. 'Hello' said Jess rather solemnly 'Hi Jess, Josie'. 'How lovely to hear your voice' responded Jess which took her mind off the conference and her concerns whether or not she would be up to do what she'd proposed. 'It's about time we met up again, are you up for it – don't tell me you're too busy?' 'Can't wait to see you Josie, when are you free, I can make it any time at the moment'. 'Tomorrow, okay with you?' 'Excellent' Jess agreed.

The next day Josie picked Jess up in her car and they travelled out to the country side for lunch. After a short while they found a lovely waterside pub down a leafy lane. The setting looked idyllic, with a garden path which wound down to the river. Josie exclaimed that she hadn't ever ventured this way before. 'This looks quite amazing shall we stop here for a spot of lunch?' Jess couldn't agree more, the surroundings looked more like paradise. After she'd parked the car they entered the pub to order lunch. Jess insisted she paid as really so appreciated Josie had kindly picked her up to drive and had managed to find this glorious place.

Both ordered a ploughman's with a glass of ginger beer, and took their lunch outside to enjoy the warm sunshine. A seat beneath the willows in the huge garden was free so sat down to enjoy the delights of the colourful garden flowers and the silent flow of the river with a small boat moored alongside.

'Gosh this looks so romantic' said a delighted Jess which prompted her to ask. 'So, what's with your love life Josie I need to catch up with what you've been up to?' 'Yes we do, said Josie between mouthfuls. 'We've both been fairly busy with work that sometimes it's a little difficult to find the time to enjoy ourselves'. 'I did hear from Jeff that you and Mike had met up for coffee some weeks ago and had had a delightful hour or two together'.

'Yes we did, it was very pleasant' said Jess 'but I'd like to know what you've been doing Josie, so please fill me in, I'm your dear friend and want to know that you're ok and happy'.

Jess did not feel like having a conversation about Mike, principally as it had been some while since they'd met up for coffee then no further word from him. He was now pushed to the back of her mind with thoughts of their friendship going nowhere.

'Well you know Peter and I started seeing each other after we'd met at College then fizzled out. Just by chance I bumped into him at our Police Headquarters some while ago and he asked me out'. So Jess immediately asked what he was doing there.

Josie continued that he too worked as a Technician but for a large hospital and he'd taken some blood samples that had been taken from a patient, a suspected criminal, to be specifically checked at our Police Laboratory.

'We've been dating now for a few weeks' Josie said. 'Oh I'm so pleased' Jess relayed 'I know you really liked him in those early days'. 'Yes' Josie continued 'I believe we have both matured since then and see life rather differently from our young student days'

Josie continued to say that they both have a lot in common besides working in similar environments. Jess sincerely hoped everything would work out fine for them both and, most importantly, to be comfortable and happy.

There's also Jeff who I've accompanied for a drink now and again. I'm not sure if he's really interested in me or if he sees me as just a colleague to keep him company when he's at a loose end. I do rather like him though.

'Wow' said Jess at this remark. 'I did think he was a nice guy, when we all met that day for dinner'. They then continued to catch up over their lunch with most of what they had been up to. Josie then reported to Jess that she had seen Mike fleetingly to speak to. 'Just a brief hello' remarked Josie 'he came into the Laboratory to get some samples checked. He did seem busy and in an awful hurry'.

'Okay' said a sullen Jess. I have been rather disappointed with him though Josie. After our last meet up he did ask if I'd mind if he kept in touch. Of course I said I would be delighted. Then nothing all this time'.

'I'm not prepared to make excuses for him Jess but I know that he's been in the process of rather a lot of criminal investigations'. Jess is interested to hear but cannot help herself being disappointed in him. Anyway she did wonder if Josie might be at liberty to explain more.

All I can tell you is that it's something to do with drug trafficking suspects. 'Oh my goodness' Jess remarked 'I imagine that could be rather dangerous'. Her friend gave a nod in response. 'I just hope he keeps safe' replied Jess in a rather nonchalant manner. Josie did not give any further information about Mike and she didn't ask.

She did not reiterate to Josie her disappointment with Mike that he'd not been in touch, which he'd stressed that he would fairly soon when they'd last met. As she'd mentioned just how busy he'd been, maybe that was his reason but not good enough as far as Jess was concerned.

However, Jess did mention that she would be away for a week with Claire in July to Ibiza and Josie had been thrilled that she would be getting away for a well-deserved break.

Now time to leave this remarkable venue, Josie took a longer route back through the beautiful countryside both with lots of small talk on their return journey. 'Thank you so much Josie, do hope we can meet up again soon' said Jess as she's dropped off at her door'. Bye Jess, have a good holiday see you when you return if not before'. Josie waved and was gone.

Chapter 19

Mike on the other hand had undergone a rather traumatic experience which involved his assistant Dan.

Deliberately he'd not contacted Jess and thrown himself into work which enabled him to give little thought to his personal life. Mike was still in a quandary about moving on with the loss of Lucy which left him powerless to dwell on Jess's feelings.

Together with colleague Dan, they'd for some time observed a likely drug trafficking ring. The suspects had been watched on several occasions as they'd hung around the gates at different schools, almost as a parent as they wait for their child. However, it had often been noticed, one of the suspects appeared to spot a very young lone teenager and follow him. This had been observed a number of times.

Mike had been told of the supposed efficiency of these men. One suspect would wait a little distance away from a genuine parent before he claimed a possible catch. Usually, another of these unsavoury characters would watch from nearby.

Their policy was to get just one child, usually a boy, from a different school each time. Mike and Dan knew precisely how drug rings worked and also had gained further information from questions put to boys who'd had an unfortunate experience with these ruthless characters..

The men, fairly smartly dressed, would approach a boy, walk alongside him and ask if he'd like to make some pocket money. Naturally, and usually, they are extremely keen and delighted to have some money. This is how they suck these innocent youngsters into their clasp.

The young boys would listen to what they were asked to do and, of course, think it very easy to get money for just delivering a package. However, they are then required, almost by force, to deliver more and more of these packages with no idea of what they contain which, of course, are drugs for onward sale.

Should the boys wish to opt out at any time, these sinister men would now have a hold on them and refused to let them go for fear they may be reported. Mike is very sure these evil characters threaten to harm their families if they do not do as they ask.

Mike and Dan, separately, have over time studied several suspects. Also followed the boys to see where they had been told to deliver the packages. Mostly to well established up market homes, buildings or warehouses.

With many discussions of their findings at Headquarters, they'd pulled together enough evidence to make an arrest. Mike, the more senior of the two, suggested Dan attempt to make conversation with one of the men first to see his reaction. 'Let's meet up at the Wooster Coffee Bar at 5pm for a chat before we make an arrest' said Mike, Dan agreed.

In the meantime, Mike at his desk with a report to write, peered at his watch and realised it was time to meet up with Dan.

Shortly before 5pm, he ordered two coffees and chose a table in a quiet corner and waited. Strange, 5.30 then 6pm Dan did not show up which was most unusual as he had never before been late.

Unbeknown to Mike, Dan had been hustled away by two armed men. While he chatted to one outside the school the suspect became suspicious of Dan and suggested they take a short walk together. A mate who was nearby immediately joined them. Then both men forced Dan into a car, covered his eyes with a scarf and drove off. Dan did not alert them as to who he was as obviously aware if he did not turn up to meet Mike as planned, the police would start a search for him.

Mike tried Dan's phone, no answer, left the Coffee Bar at 6.30pm and drove the short journey back to HQ not unduly alarmed at this stage. Maybe, for some reason, it had slipped Dan's mind to meet up at the Coffee Bar, albeit extremely unusual.

There is no sign of Dan and he hadn't reported in. Alarm bells now start to ring 'where was he?'

Mike rang Dan's home with the hope he may have contacted his wife. No, she hadn't heard from him. 'Is he ok' his wife

Judy questioned. Not wishing to alarm her Mike replied 'I'm sure he's fine, I'll get back to you when I know where he is'.

Dan would have fought these two guys off but not with a gun in his back. Fortunately, Dan had no identification on him to alert them as to who he was. In a way Dan felt pleased that he'd changed his suit that morning and accidently failed to transfer his police documents over. If only they'd known he felt sure these two men would have scarpered and released him which would have meant the police would be less likely to imminently catch them.

Now more than a little concerned Mike began to put two and two together and wondered if Dan had been a little lapse with his surveillance and been caught.

Back at HQ a plan was hurriedly put together and checks made on known drug users. Mike then sent two police officers to investigate two addresses they had on record. The officers were instructed not to mention, under any circumstances, that they had an officer missing.

The car with Dan inside had not travelled far when it came to a halt and he was forced out. One of the men grabbed him by the arm and the other pushed him violently with the gun in his back. Dan took a mental note as they walked up two flights of stairs and presumed he was in a three story house of some sort. Pushed into a room and shoved into a chair 'so what's your game mate?' questioned one of the men. Dan listened intently to the voice before he replied and played innocent replied 'I have no idea what you're talking about'. Then strung them a story that he was waiting for his son after school and his family would start to wonder where he was. For some reason it seemed they found it difficult to believe him, even though Dan was extremely good at playing down his toughness as he wanted them to believe that he was rather weak. With a, put on, shaky voice he asked that the blindfold might be removed. Of course he wished to identify them and to note exactly where he was.

They refused to do as he'd asked, but punched him instead. Dan was really angry now if only he could see. Dan heard the door close and hoped both men had left. He then struggled with his bonds, released one hand to pull down his blindfold to get an idea of where he could be.

Possibly in a three story house as first thought, and on a main street as he'd heard a lot of traffic noise. He could now hear chatter and talk of boxes being lifted and moved. .

He was right, they were boxes as he'd heard one of them say 'we need to get these packages to Jack pronto or he'll have our guts for garters now we have his money, and I know he has a number of takers'. 'Ok, let's go but we need to check on matey boy first'. Hearing this conversation Dan sat quickly back in the chair, replaced his blindfold and put both hands behind him, dropped his head as if asleep. Dan wanted to play along with them for the time being in order to find out more.

The guy, Les, checked Dan's bonds and saw they'd become loose so retied them. 'We're off now for a short while, and don't think you can escape sunshine, there will be someone here to watch you'. Damnation thought Dan.

No sooner the door closed and he wrestled with his now tightened bonds, although it took some time, he was strong and managed. Ripped off the blindfold, looked out of the window to fathom his whereabouts, although it had now become rather dark.

He very quietly turned the door knob and peeped out. Immediately a burly guy bounded towards him and Dan quickly wrestled him to the ground, and removed his gun.

Dan forced him back through the door and placed him in the chair and tied him up with the same bonds. With the gun now in his hand Dan demanded to know where the other two had gone. For fear of his life and with no clue as to who Dan was, told him they'd gone to Dales Car Warehouse.

Immediately Dan flew down the two flights of stairs, he'd carefully hidden his mobile which was on silent, and called Mike.

Overwhelmed to hear his voice and that he was ok, Mike listened to where Dan believed he was as he saw the name of the road, Princes Street, which was not too far from Police Headquarters.

Within a very short while he was picked up by a police car with a police van following and said to the driver 'we need to get to Dales Car Warehouse just follow us'. Jumped into the back of the car with Mike when he explained all that he had found out and exactly what had happened to him. 'I have to thank you Mike, you trained me well'. 'I'm just pleased that you're ok' was Mike's response.

Mike and Dan very quietly entered the Warehouse, the police van with four police officers on board, not directly on display, waited to be whistled for.

Dan kept behind Mike should he be recognised and, Mike with gun in hand, walked towards the loud voices. Dan whistled and four police officers came tearing into the Warehouse. 'You bastard' said the guy with Les as he recognised him. 'I had a feeling there was something odd about you' he exclaimed. Dan smiled and said 'sorry mate'.

They'd managed to capture all four men red-handed and forced to hand over the many boxes of packaged drugs. All four are handcuffed and put into the police van and carted off. Not forgetting, of course, the one left in the house.

After much 'no comment' from questions put to them separately, one individual opened up. They'd finally managed to secure enough evidence from him and a little from the other traffickers to bring to justice a criminal network and the mastermind behind it all.

Eventually all are charged with drug trafficking offences with a hefty prison sentence. Dan is highly commended for his part and Mike is so pleased and very happy for him.

Chapter 20

As they approached the last week of term, Jess had prepared a basic history lesson on Henry VIII as she, herself, had learned a considerable amount about this Tudor King from her own school days. However, Jess at, the last minute, reminded herself that these dear children were only 8 and 9 years old. The lesson she'd prepared, she now felt, would be a little too much of a saga for them so reduced it somewhat.

'Children today we're going to learn a little about Henry VIII and his six wives. I'm sure you've heard of this Tudor King probably because he had so many wives. So for now I suggest you make a note of the dates of the time Henry ruled and the names of his wives'.

Jess then called Ruby over to her and passed a pile of leaflets into her hand. 'Ruby would you please hand the children a copy each thank you'.

'Now children you will find there is more in the leaflet than I plan to reveal to you about Henry VIII. You'll note, when you have time to read it, a lot of the detail I will miss out on our lesson today. I will talk a little about him though which is not in the leaflet'. Jess continued. 'Perhaps one day when you are much older you may take part in a quiz and, hopefully, remember certain notes that Miss Aries relayed to you when you were in Primary School and even more once you've read the booklet. Well we hope so don't we?'

'Henry VIII was born on the 28th June 1491. His father was King Henry VII and his mother was Elizabeth of York. Henry VIII became King of England at the age of 17. He was crowned on the 24th April 1509 and ruled from that date to the 28th January 1547. He was probably the most famous of kings because he had six wives.

He had a happy childhood, when he learned sports, music and languages including Latin, French, Spanish and Greek. He was 10 years old when his older brother Arthur died at the age of 15. This meant that Henry became heir to the throne.

Henry VIII was particularly important because it was during his reign that the Church of England was created. This event was known as the English Reformation. This meant that Henry could be rid of his first wife, Catherine of Aragon, who after 24 years of marriage had not borne him a son.

Those who followed the new Church of England were named Protestants.

Before this time everyone followed the authority of the Pope in Rome known as Catholics. This is why the Church of England was set up, together with Henry and the Archbishop of Canterbury to allow Henry to be granted a divorce. This was forbidden by Rome and the Pope'.

Jess peered around her class and truly hoped they were not getting too bored with this lesson. Her class of children were, after all relatively young but she pressed on.

'I'm going to tell you a little about each of his wives. His first was Catherine of Aragon who was the wife of his older brother Arthur. She married Henry after Arthur's death in 1533. Catherine bore him a daughter, who became Mary I in 1533. This was Henry's longest marriage until he had this marriage annulled which meant cancelled or divorced.

Anne Boleyn married Henry in the same year. Although she bore him a daughter, Elizabeth (who became Elizabeth I), Henry was still determined to have a son and turned his attention to Jane Seymour. Anne Boleyn was executed on 19th May 1536 after being found guilty of treason (which meant actions which were possibly untrue) as he wanted to be rid of her to marry Jane Seymour.

Jane Seymour became Henry's third wife in 1536. She gave birth to a son in October 1537 but died two weeks later. Of Henry's six wives, she was the only one of his wives for Henry to be buried with later.

Anne of Cleves travelled from Germany to marry Henry in January 1540. Henry had been sent a portrait of her by a famous painter and did like what he saw of her. However, when she was presented to him he said "I like her not". Anne of Cleves to Henry did not look as good as her portrait. The marriage lasted for only a few weeks before he divorced her.

Kathryn Howard married Henry in 1540. She was 19 and he was 49. Their marriage was not happy and she was executed in 1542

Henry's final wife was Catherine Parr. She married Henry in July 1543. She was a very educated lady and provided comfort to Henry in his final years. She outlived Henry.

So that's a brief story of Henry VIII and his six wives. You may imagine it to be rather boring today but one day you will surely remember the story of Henry VIII that Miss Aries told you in your history lesson.

Jess observed Tommy had struggled again. She was very concerned as to how young Tommy would cope without his dear mother. It was so difficult for Jess as she felt a strong will to engulf him into her arms, to comfort him and help him so much, more than a mere teacher was allowed to do of course. 'Tommy would you like to bring your exercise book over to me'. He immediately did as he was asked.

Jess, is also concerned that the other children in her class are unaware that she is giving Tommy a little extra special attention. However, she had tried, in a few words, to explain to the children, in Tommy's absence, to be specially kind and helpful to him. Jess helped him write the details displayed on the board into his exercise book with a reminder to read the leaflet. 'Now Tommy when you are at home this evening I would like you to read what has been written down in your book and try your best to understand what we've talked about today'. 'Yes, Miss', he said. Jess then asked her class if anyone else had struggled but everyone appeared relatively happy.

Now lunchtime, Jess dismissed the class quite certain the children were more than relieved that this lesson had come to an end and with a squeeze of his hand Tommy joined them.

Chapter 21

Over the next couple of days Jess decided the children should have a wind down period before the end of term. Between classroom games, and going over what they had learned during term time, they were relaxed and happy.

The children turned up for morning class just two days before the end of term. 'Good morning children' said Jess. It was their final lesson before the start of their long summer term holiday. 'We're going to talk about the Kings and Queens of England who ruled from Henry VIII until our Queen Elizabeth who is our monarch today. This will be our last lesson before we finish for our long holiday school break.

I would like you to make a note of the name of each King or Queen and the date of the start of their reign which I have put on the board. For example Henry VIII reigned from 1509 – the next King was Edward VI from 1547. Therefore Henry VIII reigned from 1509 until 1547 which is when Edward came to the throne and so on.

Kings and Queens of England from Henry VIII - write down this title in your book.

Henry VIII 1509 : Edward VI 1547 : Jane1553 : Mary I 1553
Elizabeth I 1558 : James I 1603 : Charles I 1625 : [from 1649 – 1660 Britain became a Republic ruled by Oliver Cromwell]
Charles II 1660
James II 1685 : William III and Mary II 1688 : Mary II 1688
Anne 1702 : George I 1714 : George II 1727 : George III 1760
George IV 1820 : William IV 1830 : Victoria 1837 : Edward VII 1901 :
George V 1910 : Edward VIII 1936 : George VI 1936 :
Elizabeth II.

Well done children I can see you have all finished. We won't go into the history of these monarchs as that should be a lesson for you when you are a little older. For now, just do your best to remember the names of each King and Queen and the dates of their reign.

Apart from this lesson Jess had been unusually lenient with her class and apart from briefly going over the work they had done she ensured they do little else but try to have some fun, Jess hoped this applied to their teachers for their Maths and English lessons too.

It is now the last day of term and Jess persuaded the children to try and remember what they had learned over the past months as there may be a little test for them next term.

Jess again prompted the children 'remember to take your exercise books home with you, look at them now and again to remind you of what we have studied'. They all appeared to be keen to do just that. This was one of Jess's final remarks to her class.

Jess did spend a little time to encourage Tommy to be brave and with a few things for him to do over the holiday to try to help him cope with the loss of his mummy.

At the end of their final day 'bye my lovely children, I look forward to when I see you all again after the holiday'. Jess implied that they had been very good and helpful children and handed each of them a luxury packet of sweets to take home. 'These are for you for being wonderfully well behaved children. I'm going to miss you all and look forward to when you return next term. Now off you go home and have a happy holiday'. Of course they are all thrilled and with beautiful smiles expressed their thank you with individual goodbyes and left the classroom, even a delighted Tommy.

Jess called him over to her desk before he escaped to say another special word to him before he went home. 'Remember you will always be on my mind over the holiday and I hope you will do your very best to help Daddy as he, also, will be very sad without Mummy. You will do your best, won't you' Jess reiterated. Tommy nodded, she squeezed his hand and planted a wee peck onto his cheek, reminded him to look at his exercise book from time to time and with a little smile he skipped off with caring and loving words from his teacher.

Jess had become very fond of Tommy and truly hoped her soft words would help him get through the holiday without the little backup of support she did her best to give him on occasion.

Chapter 22

The day arrived for Jess and Claire to take their week's holiday to the Island of Ibiza. Jess had really looked forward very much to this break, although she knew she must do some work for her paper on Climate Change which was due to be presented to the Teachers' Conference in September. She had begun, however, to feel rather daunted about the prospect and whether she would be able to pull it off in a satisfactory way. Oh well, she thought, she'd got herself into this by agreement she'd better tackle it to the best of her ability somehow.

As Jess and Claire travelled to the Island of Ibiza on the rather tightly cramped aircraft, it was quite a relief when they reached their destination.

Jess had momentarily forgotten about her forthcoming ordeal as they travelled in the compact aircraft and was extremely thankful when the flight was over, and landed safely. As they descended the aeroplane steps, the warm balmy air very pleasant, with the sky a rich blue. Taken by coach, with other passengers, to their hotel where they have a room with a view overlooking the sea and the pool too looked rather spectacular.

On their first day Jess and Claire, with a shared room, went off exploring together to The Old Town an ancient sandstone fortress, built as a defence against pirates and other invaders. As they walked through the ancient gate into the city it was really rather amazing that the town had retained a timelessness about it.

The next day Jess said she would like to relax and do some written work which enabled Claire to go off and explore alone which she didn't mind at all. Over dinner the night before they had got to know other guests whom they'd travelled with. Claire relayed that she may go on a tour with a few others they'd met earlier.

The first few days were rather uneventful as friend Claire explored with other guests whom she'd befriended. This left Jess to sit alongside the pool to relax and write. Jess hoped Claire did not think her a party pooper for not accompanying her much of the time. She did, however, appear to be fine and accepted Jess did have a lot of work to do. The rest and sun a welcome escape from her busy work schedule, well would have been if she didn't have a paper to write. Claire also had a busy work schedule but she didn't have a paper to prepare which gave her more free time to explore.

Now more than half way through the holiday Jess had not seen so much of Claire who had taken a shine to one of the young male Representatives, Mark, which Jess thought was good for her as there was no sign of a boyfriend for her back home at the moment.

Jess was also pleased that she had been able to research and write a number of pages for her paper to present to the forthcoming Conference. Claire, as she had been otherwise engaged, had helped a lot, otherwise Jess would have felt more obliged to do more with her as she explored the Island.

That evening Jess decided to take a trip around the locality organised by the hotel. Claire decided to go too. Her new friend, Mark, would be involved with the tour to explain details on the way.

The evening passed most enjoyably with the added bonus of meeting some extremely friendly people from Warwick and London. They had great fun as they talked and laughed together, it was good to have Claire join in too when not giving Mark, the courier, the eye.

Thus far, Jess had kept herself very much to herself. Having rested considerably, she was now beginning to get a little bored. The following morning sat around the pool as she read her book, when 'Hi Jess, nice to see you this morning'. It was Jean and Martin, the married couple they'd met the previous evening. 'Hello so nice to see you both again. How are you?' Jess responded. 'Fine', they said in unison whilst pulling up their sun beds to place beside her.

The three of them chatted together for some considerable time when a collective 'Hello' was heard. All looked up and before them was Jack, Mark, Alan and Noel, four young men they'd met the night before as they strolled over together. All aged no more than 21 were studying at the British School of Osteopathy in London. Jack and Mark grabbed a sun bed and sat alongside them, the other two a little distance away with two young girls.

Jess then directed a question at them : 'What are you four lads doing on this quiet island when you could be having fun on the other island known for accommodating young people?' 'We didn't want to get mixed up with a lot of rowdy holidaymakers, hence we're here' replied Mark, Jack nodded in agreement.

The five of them chatted away for some time, principally about their degree course when Mark and Jack decided it might be a good idea to practice their massage techniques on both Jean and Jess, which was most welcome. A lot of the day was spent together with Jean, Martin and the boys. Well two of them as the other two seemed rather enamoured with these two lovely girls.

'We're off to the local bar tonight, why don't you come too' Mark suggested, Jack nodded again in agreement. Not imagining for one moment why they would want to be around older people. 'Yes, we'll be there' answered Jean.

After dinner that evening, Claire had said she would be off for a walk with courier rep Mark, who happened to be free that evening. Jess, of course, didn't mind at all as she, with Jean and Martin, meandered over to the pool side. 'Here they come' said Jean as she watched the boys walk over towards them. The girls we'd seen them with earlier bringing up the rear.

Mark was smartly dressed in dark trousers and shoes with a pale lemon striped shirt, very conservative for the modern day young man. 'Would you like a quick massage Jess' said Mark. 'Oh that would be very nice' Jess responded. Mark simultaneously practiced his osteopathy yet again on Jess's neck and shoulders. 'How am I doing for my 30 odd years' questioned Jess 'not bad, quite supple in fact compared with some' Mark responded. Jess felt rather pleased with that comment.

'You really enjoy your osteopathy don't you Mark'? Jess questioned. 'Yes I'm extremely interested in the skeleton and how it functions. It's something I've always wanted to explore'. Mark continued 'without the help of my parents, it would have been impossible. My brother, who is at Medical

School, and I owe them so much. I am so lucky to have such devoted and unselfish parents and one day I'm going to repay them'.

Jess continued to listen entranced and fascinated by a young man on holiday as he spoke, to a virtual stranger, so endearingly and lovingly about his parents and how they'd managed to support him and his brother through difficult times. Jess had learned from Mark earlier that his mother and biological father were divorced and it was his stepfather and his mother he had been referring to. Mark had said Dave his stepfather was more of a father to him than his real Dad ever was and would ever be. He'd continued that he regarded Dave as his father and both he and his mother were now on holiday too on the island of Fuerteventura.

Mark continued to speak deeply and affectionately about his parents so grateful to them, he was a real tonic to listen too.

'Shall we go'? Jean called. Mark finished his massaging and they left the pool side and sauntered over to the local bar at the top of the hill in a group. A warm evening, Jess with Jean and Martin sat outside on the balcony, the younger ones inside dancing to music which was played softly and not too loud.

After a short while 'come on Jess come and have a dance' Mark said at the same time wrenching her from her seat. Jess felt like his big sister, such a well-mannered likable lad full of fun with a bubbly personality. Mark had his whole life before him and one day would make a wonderful partner to a very lucky young lady. Jess and Mark had a lovely little dance together. Jess re-joined the others on the Balcony and continued to chat the night away.

'We're off to the Disco now' said Mark and Alan. Jack and Noel who'd had a little more to drink were unsure as to what they should do. 'Be careful' said Jean in her motherly tone. Although they had been drinking they were a responsible bunch and would look out for each other. 'Remember to meet up tomorrow morning at 1100am for a photo call our last whole day together' were Jess's departing words. 'Ok' raising their hands in acknowledgement they ambled off together, the other two lads dashed to join them.

Jess with Jean and Martin returned to the hotel, said goodnight and reiterated their agreement to meet up the following morning. Jess had no idea where Claire was of course but would see her later.

Snuggling down into bed Jess fell asleep almost immediately to be awoken by Claire 'Jess, Jess, Mark's dead'. Jess rubbed her eyes desperately trying to regain consciousness and most confused knowing that Claire had been seeing the local rep also named Mark. 'Claire what are you talking about, calm down' Jess responded disbelieving her words. Jess's mind was now in total turmoil, confused by the stupor of sleep.

Jess quickly realised this was no dream and struggled to pull herself together. As Claire continued her heart sank. The pit of her stomach felt weirdly hollow, an empty feeling she had never before experienced, as she realised she was talking about the lovely student Mark. Numb with shock and disbelief Jess tried to absorb her words with immediate reaction to go to him.

'It's too late' Claire blurted, they've taken him away. Apparently her courier friend Mark had been called to the scene while he and Claire were together.

Jess heard that the boys had gone to the Disco and refused to pay the extortionate entry fee so went for a walk. After a short while Mark and Alan returned to their apartment (where they occupied adjacent accommodation with the full use of the hotel's facilities). Alan went to bed, Mark not at all tired had changed into tee-shirt and shorts, hovered on their balcony to listen to music two levels above on the fourth floor. Apparently Mark was drawn towards the music, leaned backwards over the balcony, lost his balance and toppled two floors below and landed on his head. He died almost immediately.

The following morning in a state of shock Jess hurriedly dressed secretly praying there had been a dreadful mistake. Jess located Jean and Martin by the pool where she revealed the terrible news to them. For one moment she thought Jean would pass out, but quickly she regained her composure. After the initial shock, the three of them ventured into the hotel to find the boys. There they were sitting together on the sofa, no Mark! Again Jess felt this horrid pit of emptiness deep in her stomach.

'It's true isn't it'? Jess heard the words tumble from her lips. 'Yes' Jack murmured the other two poignantly quiet and subdued as they sat next to him. They were always together, now it was as if a piece of the jigsaw was missing.

'The local police are trying to locate Mark's parents, I cannot bear the thought of seeing them' continued Jack humbly. 'They will be devastated, it's just too dreadful'.

Jess hugged Jack as tears flowed down both their cheeks in a desperate attempt to keep control. Jess with Jean and Martin then left the boys as they waited for Mark's parents, not wanting to crowd them or ask questions at this time.

'You know where to find us, we're here for you' said Jean.

This the last day of the holiday, spent in total mourning for the lovely Mark, the boy Jess had met and known so briefly who'd left an indelible impression on her soul. That day, July 4th, was spent writing a letter of deep condolence to Mark's mother and Dave, the man he'd adopted as his father.

Jess relayed the spoken words Mark had uncannily shared with her the previous evening, the love that Mark had for them both, and how Jess would have been so very proud to call him her son. Jess passed the letter in a sealed envelope to Jack with a request to pass to Mark's mother and Dave. Jess had noted her telephone number should either wish to call her.

All too soon the time came for them to depart for home. The boys came hugged and waved them off with still no sign of Mark's parents. Similar to escaping a doomed ship leaving the others to their fate was a terribly sad and traumatic departure. Jess and Claire spent a very sad and mournful journey home.

A very despondent Jess and Claire had arrived home from, what was meant to be a glorious holiday with relaxation and a fun break. However it had turned out to be terribly traumatic which had overcome the enjoyable first few days they'd spent. The tragic circumstances of what had happened to the handsome adorable Mark would never leave them.

On return from their Ibiza holiday which had ended so tragically, Jess's thoughts turned to Mike. For whatever reason, why had she not heard from him? (Put him out of your mind girl. Concentrate on your conference paper, were the words that tumbled through her head).

Unable to put Mark out of her mind, nor his mother and Dave, Jess continued to wonder how his mother would be coping, how could she possibly get through this?

Two weeks passed when Jess received her first telephone call from Mark's mother Carole. Almost incoherent with grief she thanked Jess for her letter, but desperate to hear every detail of Mark's final hours and last words. There were to be many of those traumatic telephone calls which built a truly emotional bond between Mark's parents and those close to him on that holiday.

A Memorial Service was held for Mark at St Martins in the Fields in London. Many assembled from different parts of the country to honour him. The Church packed to capacity to reveal the life of a truly remarkable and lovely young man, to be torn away so tragically young and to leave such devastating emptiness for his mother and Dave's life never to be healed.

A deeply loving and caring human being so tragically and abruptly whipped away, the love of his parents trapped in a whirlpool forevermore.

Those few precious moments spent with Mark left a lasting impression, an honour to have known him and, through him, mysteriously to have spoken so lovingly of his parents on the very night he died. Mark left a remarkable emotional responsibility on Jess and others to support his parents.

The world is a poorer place without him. For those he touched during his brief life are richer by far and we are privileged to have known him.

Through this tragedy, Jess became firm friends with Jean and Martin. However, they did live some distance away and would keep in touch by telephone and to plan to meet up when their busy lives allowed.

Jess spent the next few days as she caught up with her parents and sister, Holly. She was, of course far less jovial with the loss of Mark still fresh on her mind.

Chapter 23

It had been several weeks since Jess had met up with Mike for coffee. Now most obvious to her that he could not have been as keen on her as she initially felt and he'd led her to believe. This was the conclusion Jess had reached when she'd had time to think about him occasionally.

Mike, on the other hand, had been spoken to by Jeff again to try and encourage him to move on with his life. Jeff thought he'd been a little unfair to Jess after Mike had confided in him about his conversation with her when they'd met up briefly for coffee. Jeff came to the conclusion that he'd really led Jess on, unintentionally of course, but then found it difficult to pursue their friendship.

Mike had thought very seriously about his close mate Jeff's words and eventually decided that he, at least, owed Jess an apology or an explanation and perhaps he could try and persuade her to come out for dinner if she hadn't been totally put off by his lack of contact. Also she may be dating someone else of course by now.

It was Saturday morning when 'ping' the telephone rang. Jess felt somewhat surprised to hear Mike's voice on the 'phone. 'Hi Jess forgive me for not being in touch before now, but I have been tied up with a particular case at work', was his excuse, are you alright?' 'Oh yes' replied Jess 'It's good to hear your voice after so long' she responded.

'Might you be free for us to meet up sometime?' Mike requested. Jess did not want to appear too keen as she was most put out by his lack of contact for some long while, so took a few seconds before she answered. 'Ok, would be nice to see you Mike, but I'm afraid it would have to be brief as I've so much to do'.

Jess endeavoured to work especially hard on her paper for the Teachers' Conference. Also she didn't wish to appear that keen because when last they'd met she had wondered whether Mike had led her on a little. Unless she'd read him incorrectly he'd encouraged her to believe he really liked her and would shortly be in touch to meet up again. Then, after many weeks, not one word from him until now.

All of these words were racing through her mind which made her uncertain as to whether she could trust how he truly felt about her. Oh well there's no one else in my life at the moment so just agree to go but don't get too involved, were the words racing through her mind.

'Oh gosh, I totally understand Jess, just let me know when you can manage an hour or two and I will ensure, whatever demands from my job, I will make sure and guarantee to be free for you'.

With Jess's agreement, Mike arranged to pick her up at 6pm the following evening for an early supper. He did feel a little concerned that Jess was rather adamant to keep their get together short. This made him wonder whether she did in fact, have much to do or whether she was rather hesitant as it had taken him so long to make further contact with her Whatever, he felt it was well deserved.

Jess found it not too difficult to hide her excitement when she heard his knock on the door. There before her was smartly dressed Mike in a pale blue opened necked shirt with tweed jacket and smart trousers. Jess was pleased that she had dressed smartly too in her green velvet trouser suit, which she loved, and always felt good when an opportunity arose for her to wear it.

'Hello Jess you do look lovely' said Mike 'Thank you' Jess responded in a nonchalant manner as Mike pecked her on the cheek and took her by the hand and led her to his car parked right outside.

On the way to the Restaurant Jess did not wish to relay to Mike how keen she was to see him but said 'Nice to see you Mike'. 'Oh Jess you have no idea how I felt to have the opportunity to see you again after so long'. Perhaps he really does like me Jess thought at the genuine sound of his voice, but now she was unconvinced.

They chatted comfortably together the Restaurant not too far away. Jess quickly scanned the menu and decided to have just a main course and chose salmon with baked sweet potato and roast asparagus. 'You are so healthy' said Mike as he too scrutinised the menu and chose chicken chasseur with mushrooms, green veg and mashed potato. 'That sounds delicious too' responded Jess.

As they wait for their meals, Mike took the opportunity to look at Jess and take in just how lovely she looked. Her blue eyes sparkled with delight and her smile so infectious and pretty looked genuine. Jess felt a little self-conscious at the way Mike studied her not sure if it was happiness, passion or what the hell am I doing here with his girl. However, he soon put her mind at rest as he took her hand in his and said 'thank you, I'm so pleased you agreed to see me and to come for dinner. It's been a while since we last met up together'. Mike continued 'I would have liked to explain why I hadn't been in touch but I think it can wait until the next time we have an occasion to meet, well I do hope there will be a next time'. 'Oh there's no need for you to explain Mike, I heard from Josie that you've been terribly busy'. 'Well, yes but as we have little time this evening I'd prefer to hear about you, what you've been up to and how're you're doing'.

The waiter then placed their meals before them. So between mouthfuls of delicious food, Jess opened up to Mike about her holiday with Claire. What a wonderful and relaxed time she'd experienced until the disaster happened with one of the young boys. Jess briefly explained but had no wish to dwell on it in great detail for fear of showing her utter sadness.

'I'll tell you more another time' said Jess. Mike, unbeknown to Jess, knew exactly how death can tip one over the edge so to speak. He, therefore, accepted with a nod of concern what she had to say.

'So can you tell me about your job, Mike, what do you do exactly in the police?' 'I believe you've asked me this question before Jess' Mike replied. 'I work for the CID should you have forgotten which is the Criminal Investigation Department'. Mike continued in a vague manner as he really did not wish to talk about his job at this moment in time so his reply was a little abrupt. 'I manage and conduct a range of complex investigations'. Mike is rather undefined and reticent with his reply which Jess noticed and probed no further astute enough to judge by his expression and answer not to push him more deeply with regard to his responsibilities.

Jess went on to explain her commitment and pressure to write a paper on 'Climate Change' for the forthcoming Conference. 'Oh poor you' said Mike, but I must say I feel extremely proud of you to take on such a challenge'. Jess, of course, was unaware that Mike had no interest in climate change what with Lucy's demise and his utter concentration with work which he'd thrown himself into, therefore had responded very little on the subject.

Mike said very little about his work but felt rather relaxed and happy as he listened to Jess who appeared to enjoy his company, despite his reticence to discuss his job in any detail. Nevertheless now was not a good time to get too involved.

Jess felt comfortable with him nevertheless. Although few words were spoken as to how they felt about each other, it was rather strange almost as if both knew without any words, or was this Jess's imagination. At the same time Mike was very careful after he'd heeded Jeff's words not to lead Jess on in any way. Although he did feel some keenness towards her but Lucy continued to be in his gut.

As Mike dropped Jess off at her door she declined to ask him in for coffee as the time was later than planned and she had much to do and needed to get to bed for a good night's sleep. Also she did not wish to appear too keen after he'd taken so long to make contact. Both obviously had thoroughly enjoyed each other's company though.

Jess smiled and said 'thank you Mike for a lovely evening and a delightful meal too I hope we can meet up again sometime'. 'I am concerned about the hard work you've undertaken for this conference and don't want to hinder you in any way. I would, of course, understand when next I call if you're far too busy'. Jess with a smile was a little unsure how to respond to that comment. Mike squeezed her hand, gave her a quick goodbye kiss on her cheek and was gone.

Mike sincerely hoped that he'd put the record straight with Jess as he really did like her. He found her easy to talk to - she was intelligent and pretty - he thought he would be silly to lose her so he must learn to do his best to get his act together for the future. Would Lucy understand, he must believe she would for him to continue to move forward with his life.

Jess had really quite enjoyed the short time she and Mike had spent together over dinner but, alas, it hadn't taken away her misgivings about the way he felt for her. He had, however, made her feel that he truly cared as if he would like to further their friendship.

Oh well, thought Jess, I won't lose any sleep over him just wait to see how long he will take this time before he attempts to make contact, if at all. That's how dubious Jess really felt about Mike.

PART TWO

Chapter 24

Jess began to feel a little apprehensive about the forthcoming Conference and hoped the paper she had been working on is understood and accepted by the audience. Miss Orchard, the Head Teacher at her school, had gone over the paper with Jess who thought it good and very informative. However, she explained it is difficult to know how most people feel about climate change, and global warming. Miss Orchard continued that she personally felt most strongly about the subject and anyone who is concerned should do their best to try and make most people as possible aware of the foreseeable danger of carbon emissions.

It was nice for Jess to have her Head Teacher's approval. Nevertheless, it was she who had to confront everyone with her paper on the topic.

It would soon be time for Jess to present her paper to Members of the Teachers' Conference. Jess, however, is enormously grateful that her talk is scheduled for the morning period. This will enable her to relax and listen intently to other speakers later. Jess hoped with all her heart that the number of teachers and guests in the large auditorium will enjoy her lecture.

With great trepidation she begins:

'Good morning Ladies and Gentlemen, my name is Jessica Aries. I am a Primary School Teacher. Five years ago, after my degree, I worked as a waitress for £10 an hour. During this time I was desperate to reach my goal as a teacher.

I also became very passionate about defending the natural world from destruction and joined Greenpeace. Whereby I was enlightened to document and expose the causes of environmental devastation. The work of Greenpeace is to tackle climate emergency and defend our world's biodiversity.

As you will be aware from the schedule distributed to everyone my talk is about global warming and climate change. I will, therefore, start my talk today on greenhouse gases and climate change.

Fossil fuels, as you are aware are coal, wood, oil and gas which have discharged destructive amounts of carbon dioxide into the atmosphere causing a damaging greenhouse effect which is a natural process to keep our Earth warm. The greenhouse effect is a major contribution to make Earth a comfortable place to live.

If I can explain more simply you've all heard of a greenhouse with a glass roof and glass walls for growing plants such as flowers and tomatoes, etc. A greenhouse stays warm inside, even during winter. In the daytime, sunlight shines into the greenhouse and warms the plants and the air inside. At night-time, it's colder outside, but the greenhouse stays pretty warm inside. That's because the glass walls of the greenhouse trap the sun's heat.

The greenhouse effect works much the same way on Earth. However, with all the pollution pouring into our atmosphere from the use of fossil fuels, enables the Earth to get a lot hotter and for radiation to seep through to Earth where it will eventually be less comfortable for us to live. So you see global warming is like an invisible pollution blanket around our Earth, the carbon dioxide in the atmosphere.

Climate change became a world issue three decades ago. Three decades of diplomacy has blossomed into an international consensus that the temperature rise must be curbed to "well below" 2°C (3.6°F). However in this time emissions have soared (in 1988, 20bn tons of carbon dioxide was emitted – by 2017 it was 32bn tons) with promised cuts insufficient for the 2°C goal, despite the notable growth of renewable energy such as wind and solar.

The solution is not complicated:

Eliminate the burning of coal, oil and eventually natural gas. Restrict flying to only critical, long-distance trips – in many parts of the world – trains can replace planes for short-to medium-distance trips which would help curb aeroplane emissions.

Earth's climate has been relatively stable for the past 12,000 years and this stability had been crucial for the development of our modern civilisation and life as we know it. Modern life is tailored to the stable climate we have become accustomed to. As our climate changes, we will have to learn to adapt. The faster the climate changes, the harder it could be.

Climate change is not a distant threat, it is happening now. In the past decade it has been hotter than any time in recorded history. The impacts are more evident by our extreme weather, natural disasters and chronic drought particularly in Australia.

To match the urgency of this crisis, innovative solutions are being deployed to maximise nature's ability to fight climate change – while bolstering resilience for our most precious ecosystems. Together we can halt the worst impacts and shape a better world by 2030 and beyond.

With more frequent and extreme weather events, melting glaciers, and rising sea levels, there is no question that the climate crisis is here now and the impacts are felt by humans and nature alike. However, there is good news: every day we see more individuals, organisations, businesses, and governments responding to this crisis.

People are coming together to take concrete steps to mitigate the worst impacts of climate change. By working together, we can change course. We can pave a path forward to a future in businesses to rely on renewable energy, cities to rethink waste disposal and transportation and work with communities and individuals to avoid the worst impacts of climate change. The solutions we need for a carbon-safe future already exist.

Low cost solar, wind, and battery technologies are on profitable exponential trajectories that, if sustained, will be enough to halve emissions from electricity generation by 2030. Wind and solar energy now regularly out-compete fossil fuels in most regions of the world.

Electric vehicle growth has the potential to reach a 90% market share by 2030 if sustained, but only if strong policies support this direction.

Developed responsibility, we can harness these technologies and potentially scale further unproven ones to reduce about 2/3rds of potential emissions by 2030. However, we need governments to drive this progress and take us the rest of the way.

The world is committed to fighting Climate Change! 196 countries came together in 2015 in Paris to sign the Agreement to fight the climate crisis'.

Jess continued with the importance of renewable energy in the fight against climate change.

Chapter 25

'*Renewable energy* is one of the most effective tools we have in the fight against climate change, and there is every reason to believe it will succeed.

Solar energy decreases greenhouse gas emissions which are produced when fossil fuels are burned. This leads to rising global temperatures and climate change. By going solar will reduce demand for fossil fuels, limit greenhouse gas emissions and shrink our carbon footprint.

Solar panels do not emit any greenhouse gases they use electrons which capture the sun's energy for energy creation. They derive clean, pure energy from the sun.

Tidal power: Tidal energy is created using the movement of our tides and oceans, where the intensity of the water from the rise and fall of tides is a form of kinetic (motion) energy. Tidal power surrounds gravitational hydropower, which uses the movement of water to push a turbine to generate electricity. The turbines are likened to wind turbines, except they are positioned underwater. Hydropower is completely renewable, which means it will never run out unless the water stops flowing.

Hydropower is a clean, renewable, and environmentally friendly source of energy. It contributes significantly to the reduction of greenhouse gas emissions and to the security of the energy supply.

Tides are predictable and constant, thanks to gravitational forces. With the need to assess the low or high tide, makes it easier for engineers to design efficient systems.

One of the more modern hydropower innovations is 'tidal energy' or 'offshore hydropower'. This involves harnessing the power of the changing tides of the sea to generate energy to turn into electricity. Tidal power turbines are often placed in shallow waters off the coast and as the tides flow in and out, the water flowing back and forth passes through large turbines powering a generator.

Chapter 26

Deforestation is when forests are cleared. We are not only knocking out our best ally in capturing the staggering amount of greenhouse gases we humans create, primarily by burning fossil fuels at energy facilities, and of course, in cars, planes and trains

Also cutting down trees, when felled, they release into the atmosphere all the carbon they have been storing. After trees are felled they are either left to rot or they are burned which creates further emissions. Deforestation alone causes about 10% of world-wide emissions.

Forests are crucial in the fight against global warming by absorbing carbon from the air. We need to protect the forests that are home to well over half the world's land-based species of plants and animals. They have a vital role to play in the fight against global warming.

What to do? We need to plant trees on land where forests have been cut down and encourage people to live in a way that does not harm the environment.

Kelp and Underwater Forests: Research has found that per acre, kelp forests can absorb up to 20 times more carbon dioxide from the atmosphere when compared to land-based forests. Globally, these underwater kelp forests absorb roughly 600 million tonnes of carbon per year almost twice the annual carbon emissions of the UK.

Kelp is the name given to large brown algae seaweeds, which often accumulate into dense groups known as "kelp forests". These extensive underwater habitats range along 25% of the world's coastlines, and are one of the most productive and biodiverse ecosystems on Earth.

Kelp grows at an extraordinary rate, up to 2ft in a single day: seaweeds can grow more than 30 times faster than land-based plants.

A kelp forest once stretched along 40km of the West Sussex coastline and 4km out to sea. Unfortunately, within the last few years, these kelp forests have almost completely disappeared, with only a few pockets remaining. Reasons for this decline include changing fishing practices and the dumping of sediment close to the shore which blocks light and limits the kelp's ability to grow.'

Sir David Attenborough stated "The loss of the Sussex kelp forests over the past 40 years is a tragedy. We've lost critical habitat that is key for nursery grounds for water quality and for storing carbon".

'Fortunately there is a campaign to restore the kelp forest to restrict trawling along the Sussex coastline year-round. A decision made after the "Help Our Kelp Campaign" received overwhelming support after featuring a documentary. The film showcased Sussex's kelp forest decline, and the importance of its conservation.

Kelp forests throughout the world play an important role. Predictive experiments suggest that Arctic coasts are in line to become one of the most impacted environments in the world under changing climate. Yet the possible expansion of kelp forests should provide new habitats for fish and other marine organisms, and enhance a suite of valuable ecosystem services along Arctic coastlines.

Chapter 27

Cars and Global Warming: Passenger vehicles are a major pollution contributor, producing significant amounts of nitrogen oxides, carbon monoxide, and other pollution. In 2013, transportation contributed more than half of the carbon monoxide and nitrogen oxides, and almost a quarter of the hydrocarbons emitted into the air.

Cleaner vehicles and fuel technologies can provide us with an affordable means of reducing transport related air pollution and climate change emissions. Electric cars and larger vehicles can entirely remove exhaust emissions.

It is reported that electric charged vehicles reduce emissions as they emit less greenhouse gases and air pollutants than a petrol or diesel car. Once an electric vehicle hits the road the bulk of its emissions have already been produced, whereas with combustion engines, a long period of exhaust emission production is just beginning.

Oil Drilling: Drilling for oil, both on land and at sea, is disruptive to the environment and can destroy natural habitats. When oil and gas is extracted, the voids fill with water, which is a less effective insulator. This means more heat from the Earth's interior can be conducted to the surface, causing the land and the ocean to warm.

Our use of oil is also one of the biggest contributors to climate change - only coal has a greater impact. Oil also poses a direct threat to communities near extraction sites and pipelines. Major oil spills have polluted oceans and coastlines for decades after. Smaller leaks gush from active pipelines almost every day. These spills poison land and water supplies, and pose a health risk to people living nearby.

The simple fact is: we don't need more oil. Advances in electric vehicles and improved transport network mean we can do without. It is shown that we can reduce the amount we use through clean energy and better transport. The good news is people around the world have stopped oil giants from drilling in fragile environments.

Flooding: Warm air can hold more water vapour than cold air. For each 1°C rise in temperature air can contain about 7% more moisture, which can condense to fall as rain as a consequence.

More than 70% of the planet's surface is water, and as the world warms more water evaporates from oceans, lakes, rivers and soils.

Climate change affects coastal flooding through sea level rise. Global warming is causing sea levels to rise. First, glaciers and ice sheets worldwide are melting and adding water to the ocean. The volume of the ocean expands as the water warms. The water warms through sunlight. Clouds, water vapour, and greenhouse gases emit heat that they have absorbed, and some of that heat energy enters the ocean. Heat energy in the ocean can warm the planet for decades after it was absorbed.

Permafrost - The Arctic: Polar ice caps are melting as global warming causes climate change. We are losing Arctic sea ice at a rate of almost 13% per decade. Over the past 30 years, the oldest and thickest ice in the Arctic has declined by a stunning 95%.

(2020 was the hottest year on record, will 2021 be worse?).

If emissions continue to rise unchecked, the Arctic could be ice-free by the summer of 2040. However what happens in the Arctic does not stay in the Arctic. Sea ice loss has far-reaching effects around the world.

Other changes are happening in the Arctic. In Canada, Alaska, Greenland, Norway and Siberia, permafrost soils that have been frozen for thousands of years are receding by half a metre per year. Thawing permafrost and crumbling Arctic coasts are dumping sediments into coastal waters at alarming rates, which blocks light and could limit plant growth.

Polar Bears: Melting ice is affecting Polar Bears who will soon starve to death. These bears need to eat 60% more than anyone first realised. Polar Bears' utter dependence is on seals for their food. They need food with a high content of fat and that makes seals their ideal prey.

With the Arctic ice breaking up, it will become more difficult for the Polar Bears to capture their prey. They sit near the breathing holes and wait for the seals to pop up for air. Without sea ice, bears won't be able to catch any seals and will subsequently starve to death.

A new study has predicted that most polar bears in the Arctic will become extinct by 2100 if greenhouse gas emissions remain on their current trajectory. Further, polar bears are likely to experience reproductive failure by 2040, reducing the number of offspring needed for population maintenance.

Polar bears can be saved through habitat protection, unlike other species threatened by hunting and deforestation. Reducing greenhouse gas emissions on a global scale will help deter some of the negative effect of the climate crisis, and will subsequently assist in maintaining sea ice integrity, preventing sea levels from rising and ensuring polar bears are able to feed and nourish themselves as well as their cubs'.

Chapter 28

Oceans: 'The Ocean is the largest living space on earth and two thirds of it is owned by no one. How do we protect such a place so vast? The high seas are so large, deep and dark.

Phytoplankton plants in the deep oceans are so dense and amazingly extensive they can be seen from space. Plankton so numerous they create more oxygen than the world's forests and grasslands combined. Plankton soak up massive quantities of carbon, a crucial ally in our fight against climate change.

How does one protect phytoplankton? They have a tendency to sink to the bottom of the ocean where no plant can grow. Enter the whales, the whales mix up the water flicking the sinking plankton back into the sunlight.

They defecate at the surface, fertilising the sunlit shallows and fuelling the growth of plankton. The plankton feeds fish and krill and the fish and krill feed whales. The whales then recycle the nutrients back to where they are most needed. So for the plankton to survive it's the predators who need protecting.

Waste: We now have a new threat, our waste washed off the land, it never really disappears. By 2050 there could be a greater weight of plastics in the ocean than fish. As it fragments it is ingested by plankton works up the food chain and then accumulates in the bodies of the top predators. So how can we protect the high-seas and better control of what we take out and what we put back in?

Currently only 1% of the high seas are protected we could set aside a third or more as Sanctuaries where all marine life can thrive. We can all play our part in saving the highs seas by seeking out products that never need to be binned. Where everything is designed to last and never discarded but recycled.

There is hope right now with The United Nations negotiating a brand new Treaty to protect all life in the high seas'.

"We once thought the oceans were too vast to be polluted too bountiful to be depleted, we still act as if the high seas belong to no one. It's time to embrace that they belong to us all. This is our opportunity to restore what we have lost to protect all the wonders of the high seas and to choose products fit for a finite planet for *OUR PLANET*" said David Attenborough [1]

'An international group of scientists said that if the planet's temperature rises by more than 1.5°C, it will cause huge problems for the planet. It doesn't sound very much but enough to cause massive devastation.

No country can deal with this alone. All countries need to work together to limit the rise in temperature to 1.5°C and stop changes to the planet that would be catastrophic for life on Earth.

Furthermore, climate scientists say that for serious change to happen, everyone on the planet must try to help:

(a) Stop burning fossil fuels by the middle of this century.

(b) Plant more trees

(c) Protect forests

(d) Develop machines to suck carbon out of the air.

This could help the most serious effects of climate change and stop global temperatures rising above 1.5°C.

Armed Conflicts: Governments need to understand how armed conflicts harm the environment. Critically, environmental damage has implications for people as well as ecosystems. This means protecting civilians which first requires that we protect the environment they depend upon.

High intensity conflicts require and consume vast quantities of fuel, leading to massive CO^2 emissions and contributing to climate change.

The use of explosive weapons in urban areas creates vast quantities of debris and rubble, which can cause air and soil pollution.

Severe pollution incidents can be caused when industrial oil or energy facilities are deliberately attacked, inadvertently damaged or disrupted. In some cases, deliberate attacks on oil or industrial facilities are used as a weapon of war, to pollute large areas and spread terror.

Systems often break down during conflict leading to increased rates of waste dumping and burning, improper management and less waste segregation.

Over 20% of the world's population live in conflict-affected areas and fragile states.

War and armed conflict present a risk for humanity and other forms of life on our planet. Too many lives, and species, are at stake'.

"United Nations urge everyone to renew their commitment to jealousy. Protect our planet from the debilitating effects of war and especially at a time our warming planet is already threatened by the impacts of runaway climate change".

Chapter 29

'*Scandinavia*: is showing the world how to live well in an eco-friendly way. Climate change is happening now. The question is: can we deal with it before it is too late?

Just off the coast of Svalbard are a cluster of islands covered in ice and snow which are in the Arctic Ocean halfway between mainland Europe and the North Pole.

The surrounding area covered by ice and snow is almost like another planet. At certain times of the year the sun never gets above the horizon. Although it is so far North people do live there. The largest town is home to roughly 2,000 inhabitants and is as far North as anyone lives on the entire planet. How does climate change affect people's lives there?

Firstly, it is a legal requirement to carry a rifle when away from the small town, as a protection, to scare off the Polar Bears. By comparison the biggest threat to people in London is the Congestion charge.

The temperature in Svalbard has risen by more than 6°C in just 50 years. This means the permafrost is melting and buildings are cracking because they have not needed a solid foundation in the past.

Temperatures are rising so fast that large parts of this town are being rebuilt with deeper foundations.

Although Svalbard is part of Europe it is on the front line of climate change. This island is almost half the size of England.

Around two thirds of these islands are covered by glaciers. The rising temperatures there are affecting the entire planet. The glaciers are melting and retreating and thinning the melting arctic ice which is leading to sea levels rising across the world. As the climate warms, it sets off a chain reaction causing the planet to warm even faster.

Copenhagen: Europe is leading the way in global effort to reduce carbon emissions and even by European standards Denmark is green. Copenhagen has gone even further it is planning to be carbon neutral by 2025 showing us all. So how are they doing it?

Their Power Plant does not run on fossil fuels but has been replaced by rubbish. If all of the rubbish was put in landfills instead, it would emit greenhouse gases as the waste rots. Most residents in Copenhagen recycle to reduce emissions, the impact is instant.

With solar powered electricity and boats too. With everyone riding around the city on bicycles, using electric boats and also canoeing, they will hit their carbon neutrality by 2025.

In spite of all this, it is felt that the challenges of the future are not being taken seriously enough.

Although one of the greenest cities in the land, but to be generally carbon neutral, we are all going to have to think very hard about how much we consume in many ways.

Sweden: Each Friday, students stand outside Parliament to put pressure on the Government politicians to act against climate change. They are demanding the reduction of greenhouse gas emissions to zero. It is a huge request but needs to be done.

In a democracy public opinion is what runs society, so if enough people become aware and decide that we are going to do something, then we can achieve. These young people believe and are stating so in desperate terms.

Climate change realisation has spread to more than 100 countries. These young people are fired up and hungry for change and for the first time feel like change might be coming. That the world may finally be waking up to what is at stake.

What is climate change? When it is questioned it's mentioned about global changes in the Earth's average temperature which moves up and down naturally but it has been increasing more rapidly than usual.

This change is impacting on the planet's environment - which is everything natural around us - rivers, trees, plants, animals …….everything!

What causes climate change? A lot of people consider climate change the most important crisis that the world is facing today; but what is it?

Why are so many scientists, campaigners and politicians concerned about its effects? It is a complicated issue but a very important one.

One of the reasons why scientists believe that climate change is caused by humans this is because the planet's environment has changed dramatically since an era of history known as the Industrial Revolution.

The Industrial Revolution was a period of history when humans started creating factories and machines to make lots of products quickly and cheaply.

Burning of Oil, Coal and Gas (Fossil Fuels) are used to power factories, buildings and transportation. When burnt substances are released into the atmosphere it's called carbon dioxide, which traps heat from the sun and warms up the Earth, namely the Greenhouse effect.

Waste: The way waste is disposed of often adds to harmful emissions. Even food waste creates greenhouse gas called methane when it rots.

Deforestation and Urbanisation: When more people start living in cities, urbanisation is when a forest or tree-covered area is turned into something else. (For example, a farm or space for houses).

Trees help us by absorbing carbon dioxide – but they release it back into the air again when they are cut down.

Scientists say the world is about 1°C warmer than it was 300 years ago when the Industrial Revolution started and people began to work in factories.

The children in my class have been very interested to learn a little about fossil fuels and their history. I am alerting them in a gentle way about our planet and what is happening as they are our future and will be left to deal with the aftermath'.

Chapter 30

'I would now like to move on to plastics particularly plastic bags'.

"At first there is no obvious connection between the Siberian tiger, the snows of Kilimanjaro and a plastic bag. Two of them inspire awe.

Even if we never see a tiger in the wild or climb to the top of Africa's highest mountain and touch the ice cap, we feel our lives are somehow enriched by their existence - but the plastic bag? At best it is occasionally convenient. At worst, it is a serious threat to the environment, and that is the link - the environment.

All three of them are symbols, but in one vital respect the plastic bag is the most powerful of the three. Here's why!

The Siberian tiger – perhaps the most awesome predator on the planet - once freely roamed the forests of north-eastern China, the Korean peninsula, Mongolia and Russia.

Today, there may be as few as 350 left in one small corner of south-eastern Russia. The battle for its survival may well be lost. So it is with Kilimanjaro.

There is no more magnificent image on the African continent than its brilliant white peak rising 20,000ft above the sun-scorched plains. But the ice cap is melting at such a rate that most scientists believe it will have disappeared in little more than ten years. A few decades of global warming will have destroyed what was created 11,000 years ago.

Now let us turn to the ravages of the plastic bag. They are everywhere. No one knows for sure how many were given away by shops and supermarkets around the world, but it has been estimated at a million a minute. In these small islands alone it was a staggering 13 billion every year. We used them once or, perhaps, twice if our kitchen bins were lined with them. The vast majority were simply thrown away.

You would find them stuck in the trees and bushes of your park, blown across the playground of your school, or shoved into landfill. You cannot escape them.

In the unspoiled Peloponnese, (the southernmost part of mainland Greece) the loveliest corner of Europe, you can sometimes be lucky enough to watch dolphins playing in the waters of the bay. The beaches are free of pollution – except for plastic bags.

Given certain wind and tides the coastline can be disfigured overnight by tons of plastic waste, forming a foul necklace around every bay for miles. Almost all of it comes from plastic bags, many of which have been in the sea for years. They are torn and shredded, but the plastic of most of them is virtually indestructible.

At least the beaches can be cleaned, the plastic painstakingly plucked from them. You cannot do that to the sea. The hidden menace of old plastic bags is far greater than the visible one. They are swallowed by marine life from the Arctic to the Antarctic – mammals and birds. Marine conservationists reckon that they kill 100,000 whales, seals dolphins and turtles every year.

A whale washed up on a beach in France had dozens of plastic bags tangled in its intestines – including two from British supermarkets.

So the plastic bag kills precious wildlife as surely as the environmental vandals who fell the forests of Asia or slaughter tigers to sell their body parts to be used in imaginary 'cures'.

They also play their pernicious part in the global warming that is melting the ice cap of Kilimanjaro and represents a threat to the survival of our planet. Man-made global warming is predominately the result of carbon released into the atmosphere – mostly from oil and what is needed to make every plastic bag? *Oil*: Although a discarded piece of filthy old plastic does not exactly provide the emotional jolt of a magnificent animal such as the Siberian tiger or a breath-taking mountain peak in Africa, it can deliver a message that is even more important It can tell us that our destiny is in our own hands We can do something. We need to make the world aware of the devastation of plastic materials. Each year, more than 8million tons of plastic enter the world's oceans".*[1]

'In 1992 a container ship, travelling from Hong Kong, lost one of its containers in a storm. It was carrying 28,000 plastic ducks. Since then the ducks have travelled more than 17,000 miles some landing in Hawaii and even spending years in an Arctic ice pack.

In 2003 and 2007 they even arrived on the shores of the UK as well as South Africa and Australia. This story is told to realise how plastic can travel about the globe's sea, kill marine life, marine animals, including whales and turtles, often consume this plastic by accident and become sick or die as a result. Plastic can last forever as it is not easily degradable.

Lead the way to a Plastic Free Future.

In the end, this is about more than plastic bags or plastic toys – or tigers or ice caps. In some ways they are equivalent of the canary in the coalmine falling off its perch. If the miners fail to notice, they will pay the price.

But, just for a change, let's take a more optimistic approach and give the final word to Shakespeare. In "Julius Caesar", he wrote: "There is a tide in the affairs of men which, taken at the flood, leads on to fortune". If we can deal with the tide of plastic bags, who knows what else we can do?'

Chapter 31

'Before continuing, I'd like to briefly mention China and Finland.

China: remains the world's largest greenhouse gas emitter and produces 28% of the world's emissions – more than the United States and Europe combined. However, the Chinese Government states that China would become carbon neutral by 2060.

Finland: is ranked the least polluted country in the world.

The Solomon Islands: I think it is important to mention these islands as it is quite catastrophic as to what is happening there.

Climate change has made entire islands disappear as sea levels rise salt water sweeps inland, eventually killing the trees. Without trees to hold the sand in place, islands would end up washed away.

Sea levels have risen between 15-20 centimetres. Although it does not seem a lot, it has a dramatic impact on the vegetation. Several islands are now completely under water.

Even if we stopped pumping carbon dioxide into the air tomorrow, the warmer temperatures we have already created will cause sea levels to continue to rise for the next 100 years.

One should not become complacent about climate change because it is happening somewhere faraway, it is devastating to witness islands literally crumbling away into the sea. We must realise time is running out if we do not act now.

Heron Island: The Great Barrier Reef is one of the wonders of the world, bursting with marine life with hundreds of corals and more than a thousand species of fish, including some of the larger ones. This Island is a breeding spot for the underwater world's most incredible creature, the Green Turtle.

Turtles are so important for the marine eco system helping to keep sea life in balance. However, they lay their eggs on the beach and, as the world warms up, the sand is warming too and that becomes a huge problem.

The WWF is working out ways in which to cool the sand temperature, as sand temperatures are determining the sex of the hatchlings. For the Northern Great Barrier Reef, Green Turtles over the last 10-20 years have produced 99% female. If this trend continues for decades to come that will irreversibly lead them towards extinction.

Therefore the turtle eggs are being collected and kept cool in the hope that more males will hatch. It would be good if humans did not have to intervene in this process. The issue at the moment is the change in temperature, due to climate change, which is happening so rapidly that our environment is unable to adapt fast enough.

Green turtles' behaviour has not changed over thousands of years. Temperatures are rising so quickly there is no time for the turtles to change, or adapt, their behaviour it's necessary for humans to intervene to help.

Australia: is the biggest exporter of coal in the world, perhaps that's why a lot of their people are sceptical about climate change.

In rural Queensland around November 2019 about 1/3rd of this huge country was in drought. A sheep farmer should have been surrounded by acres of lush green grass and would normally have up to 8,000 sheep. However, with hardly any rain he could only afford to keep 1,000.

When driving out to feed the sheep it is a rocky, barren waste land which appears more like a desert. With no grass for the sheep to feed on the farmer would pay up to £400 per week for corn, their water supply just one small puddle which the sheep could not possibly survive on.

It was expressed that, apparently, this is far and beyond a drought, but a disaster and the worst man has ever experienced in this country. "There is definitely something happening to the climate", stated the farmer, "which cannot be denied". They do not get the rainfall or the spring rainfall which was abundant. It is very obvious that change is happening and slowly destroying the land. Farmers are almost in tears with what appears to be a national disaster in a rich and prosperous country struggling to cope by how hard it has been hit by climate change.

East coast Australia has always had bush fires but the drought has been making the fires more intense.

For miles and miles everywhere is blackened and scorched by bush fires. The fire devastation over a massive area is incredibly worrying. This is what Australia must deal with day in and day out over many months.

With such dry ground and a slight wind, a small fire can change into a raging inferno. An area larger than England has gone up in smoke with thousands of homes burnt.

Australians are now saying we must stop burying our heads in the sand, people must step up and learn from this. More and more people are realising the threat of climate change. However, in Sidney, on a beautiful and clear day, the troubles of the countryside can feel a very long way away'.

'While on the continents of Australia we should mention the beautiful island of

Tasmania: It's lush green, cold and damp and leading the way to find solutions for climate change. The waters around this island have something in them that could help save our planet.

These waters are home to one of the solutions of carbon dioxide which is giant kelp. As it grows, it sucks up carbon dioxide and stores it away as a forest of plants, not on land but under water.

The giant kelp is one of the fastest growing plants on the planet and can capture carbon more quickly than in rain forests. It can actually grow up to 40-50 centimetres a day and the uptake of carbon is just fantastic. Of course then all of that carbon gets stored in the biomass of the kelp forest.

Unfortunately, the giant kelp is struggling and dying because of the warmer water temperatures.

A team of researchers in Tasmania are placing more resilient kelp, which can survive in warmer temperatures, under water. A team dive down and plant a string of tiny little kelp, which are almost microscopic, and place the tiny kelp deep down in the water and within 12 months, probably 8 months, this kelp will be 10 meters long.

The kelp, however, does face another threat. Due to the warmer sea temperature, has enabled thousands of millions of sea urchins to survive which feed on the kelp. So to give the kelp a fighting chance, the sea urchins have to go.

In the last 12 months 560 tons of sea urchins have been harvested. There is an industry taking this up as people are being encouraged to eat them. Apparently the sea urchin has a lot of nutritional benefits.

Moving further on into Tasmania an academic wrote and gave speeches around the world on climate change. His, and many others' view is, there's a reasonable chance of a catastrophic impact globally. How bad could it get is very clear from the scientific evidence of the possibility of total collapse of global civilisation as absolutely a possibility. The path we are on today is the most likely outcome.

It's really difficult to imagine going from our world of plenty to the total collapse of civilisation. However, it is completely solvable. There is nothing basically that we cannot fix. There is no technological limitation, no economic limitation and no lack of wealth, or lack of intellectual innovation that we have to stand in the way of fixing this completely.

We must eliminate the burning of fossil fuels - coal, oil and gas to be gone inside 10 years. The economy must be transformed in that way in a decade. Governments will do this if forced to do so by the public who must put on pressure

It is not too late because we have an amazing capacity to do things extraordinarily quickly. Every bit of technology we need to get ourselves off of fossil fuels is available today.

In Tasmania they are already getting close with wind farms still under construction powering 60,000 homes. This wind farm will enable the island to reach a major mile stone producing all of its electricity from renewable sources and it's not stopping there. They can export power to the mainland of Australia. Tasmania will be the powerhouse of Australia.

This island is an exciting glimpse of what we can do if we put our minds to it.

The question is whether we can do what Tasmania is doing across the entire planet'.

Jess now brought up the Paris Agreement:

'Edmonton – Canada: In 2015, 196 States signed up to the Paris Agreement to limit global temperature rise to well below 2°C and to pursue efforts to keep it to 1.5°C. The Agreement

aims to substantially reduce global greenhouse gas emissions in an effort to limit the global temperature increase this century

The Canadian Oil and Gas industry employ 170,000 and contributes over $70M a year to the country, but it is also the largest contributor to Canada's greenhouse gas emissions. The potential trade-off between the strength of the economy and the health of the planet is a story repeated around the world.

It is destroying so many people's lives and so much natural habitat. Things must change.

Average temperatures in Canada have risen by 1.7°C, twice as fast as the rest of the world. For instance take the Jasper National Park.

A rise in temperature has allowed a pest to flourish and attack the pristine Pine Forest leaving these trees defenceless and a huge number are dying.

The beetles get under the bark, eat the tissue to get inside the gallery and lay their eggs. When the larvae hatch, they feed on the tissue the tree uses to transport its nutrients. Effectively, the tree dies. About 50% of the forest has been affected.

These beetles have never before caused such wide spread devastation as freezing winter temperatures normally kill them off. ⁻40°C is usually the norm, but over the last decade the winters have not been cold enough to kill off the beetle'.

Chapter 32

Jess continued with her lecture, again hoping against hope that she can continue to hold her audience attention. 'I would like to say a few words about Earthquakes and the possible devastation that they can or may cause.

Earthquakes that generate tsunamis happen most often where Earth's tectonic plates converge and the heavier plate dips beneath the lighter one. Part of the seafloor snaps upward as the tension is released. The entire column of sea water is pushed toward the surface, creating an enormous bulge causing a tsunami

The 2004 Boxing Day tsunami was caused by a powerful under sea earthquake. The quake created the ocean floor to suddenly rise by as much as 40 meters which triggered a massive tsunami.

The tsunami lasted for just 10 minutes but generated utter devastation and many deaths as they can move as fast as a jet plane, over 500mph (800km/h), and can cover entire oceans in less than a day. A tsunami can reach the coast in 30 minutes.

Slight sea level rises linked to climate change could significantly increase the devastating effects of massive tidal waves like a tsunami.

I've explained a little about Earthquakes I do hope you won't mind if I relay some personal stories about the tsunami which occurred on December 26th 2004 and the dreadful aftermath and devastation for some holiday makers. I do hope it does not distress you, as much as it did me, to hear these stories. Of course we all heard about it at the time as it was the most devastating in our history'.

Jess continued: 'At 7.59am a 9.1 magnitude earthquake - one of the largest ever recorded – ripped through an undersea fault in the Indian Ocean, propelling a massive column of water toward unsuspecting shores.

A family had been 3 days into their holiday in Khao Lak Thailand and were standing around the swimming pool when they started to hear a terrible noise. No one recognised the sound you could almost believe that it was in one's mind. It felt like the Earth was coming apart but everything looked perfectly normal. As the family stood on the beach and faced towards the sea a huge black wall was seen coming towards them which looked nothing like the sea. They were just as suddenly all swept away. There was no warning'.

'I would now like to mention Rosie who shared her story much later which left her an orphan.

Rosie was just 8 years old at the time of the 2004 Boxing Day Tsunami. Her parents had taken her and her three brothers, aged 12, 15 and 17 on holiday to Sri Lanka and they were staying in an apartment on the beach front in a town called Weligama.

It was early on December 26th when the water began streaming into their room. The first water came in and her father tried to hold the door. Then the big wave followed after. Her mother helped Rosie out while her father searched for her brothers, but at that point her father was washed out of the room. She did not know what happened to him afterwards. Rosie's mother managed to hold on to her and got her out of the apartment clutching her in a secure lifeguard position. Rosie's mother got her out but they were now in open water. Her mother, unfortunately, couldn't hold on any longer and went under.

Separated from her mother, Rosie managed to hold on to a tree. She recalled being pulled by the water for what felt like an eternity as her hair got caught on debris. She was able to scramble for air after ripping her hair away.

Rosie swam over to some bars on a house, and managed to cling on to them for dear life and climb up. From where she clung on she screamed all her family member names but no one was around. Then she had to think about herself, get down and chance it.

She managed to make her way to some train tracks nearby and found herself surrounded by Sri Lankans who couldn't understand her, and vice versa, due to the language barrier. Rosie followed a line of people with no idea of where she was going until a man, who did speak English, spotted her and saw that Rosie was covered in cuts on her arms, back and foot. He took her to the top of a hotel and from there the British Embassy was contacted.

Rosie was in this hotel for a very long time before someone told her that her brothers were at the bottom of the stairs. She said it was the best moment of her life – with all her injuries she ran over into their arms and they all hugged. She said it was amazing that they had found each other.

Two of her brothers had managed to hold onto the roof of a building while her other brother was found up a coconut tree, said Rosie. The children returned to where they had been staying but could not find their parents.

Rosie was badly injured and one of her brothers suffered from asthma, so they needed to get home and get help.

From Weligama the four hitchhiked to Columbo international airport. They boarded a flight home to England and were reunited with the rest of their family. Rosie's older 21 year old sister adopted her siblings.

Rosie remembered walking through the airport with no shoes. They were taken aside given some clothes and taken to hospital. Back in the UK they were given so much support from family and friends and from fundraising. Sadly, however, they had lost their parents'.[1]*

Chapter 33

Jess continued with other stories:

'On holiday in Khao Lak, Thailand: A family were having breakfast at the hotel on a terrace, overlooking the pool, the beach and the sea. Husband Tom noticed the waiters were all pointing out to sea which was receding rapidly. It was a fascinating sight. People retrieved their cameras and walked towards the dry seabed. The beach was full of sunbathing tourists.

Tom had an uncomfortable feeling though. He had lived for two years on the beach in California and had never seen a sea behave in this way. Then it clicked: the trembling he had heard earlier was an earthquake. The receding water was the prelude to a tidal wave.

Tom grabbed his wife's hand and screamed, 'Run!'. At that same moment, he saw a high wall of water come crashing over the reef towards them at a speed of 40-50mph. They ran uphill fast. The water was right behind them. The noise was deafening.

Tom looked behind and saw the beach and pool area were a boiling mass of water. Palm trees, beach chairs and parts of bungalows were twirling around and people were frantically trying to hold on to anything. They continued to walk towards higher ground, up the steep hill into the jungle beyond and waited for two hours, with the knowledge that very few people would have survived the onslaught below.

When the sea looked calm again they descended to the hotel, and found many badly wounded people. They helped get them on to the back of trucks taking the injured to hospital.

Warned another tsunami was on its way they climbed up into the jungle again, where they waited for three more hours.

The family eventually came down the hill where there were cars and trucks loaded with many injured. No one knew what to do or where to go. They were reluctant to walk down to the lower level as all those who hadn't survived would be scattered all along the beach.

The next day the road was clear, and the family could then start the long trip home. The floor of the bus station was covered with wounded people, all waiting for the bus to Bangkok. People were almost in tears, at the opportunity to use the family's cell phone, to reach their families that they were alive.

The guilt was hard to bear. Tom could never forgive himself for not going to the hospital to help the injured, particularly to return home unscathed when so many had lost their lives'.[1]*

Chapter 34

A couple snorkelling on Phi Phi Lei, Thailand)

They'd won a snorkelling trip in a raffle on Christmas Eve at their hotel, Phi Phi Charlie on Koh Phi Phi. That raffle saved their lives.

They had been snorkelling in the water when the Thai guides started to call everyone back onto the boats. The water had receded rapidly from the shoreline and nobody knew what was happening. They were lucky and managed to get back onto the boat as the waves came in, and the boat swiftly repositioned itself some few hundred metres away from the coast. However, as strange currents began to develop and the waves started to impact upon the bay, they witnessed many people being swept away.

Long-tail boats that had been closer to the shoreline snapped and sank like twigs. They couldn't believe how lucky they were to get back onto the boat. The couple didn't know what had happened to the people they'd been snorkelling with or if they'd been swept away.

Just imagined some localised freak incident had taken place but 30 minutes later the boat guides had a phone call from friends who said Phuket and Phi Phi Don had been hit badly by a tsunami.

It became clear that Koh Phi Phi, where they'd been staying, was devastated by the waves. The hotel was destroyed, and only recently heard that over half the people staying there were killed. They remained in open water for the rest of the day waiting for more advice about what to do.

It wasn't until late afternoon that the boat took them back to Koh Phi Phi Don. It was then that the tragedy became apparent.

On return they sailed into a soup of debris from the island which included TVs, fridges, holiday books and worse. It was just awful, and obvious to see the island was devastated and the infrastructure shattered.

One man on board had a mobile phone when everyone in turn attempted to call home to say they were safe.

All decided to stay on the boat that night, moored out at sea. The boat was too small to have taken everyone all the way to Phuket. The only option was to wait for help to arrive in the morning. It was the longest night of their lives and if it had not been for the camaraderie of those passengers on board and the wonderful generosity of the Thai people who owned and manned the boat, it would have been unbearable.

As the sun rose, the boat was taken into the harbour once again and waited for the larger boats to arrive. It was just awful. Witnessed from their position on the water one could see hundreds of people all desperate to get off the island. They were huddled together on the pier in the harbour.

Eventually the family got the ferry boat to Phuket that morning and after a long wait boarded an army plane back to Bangkok and a flight home.

All of their possessions had been lost but were not concerned just eternally grateful to be alive. It was an awful situation and such a random tragedy. Why did they take that boat trip that day? What if they'd overslept? Why should they be the ones to survive and not so many others like them who didn't, it is senseless and random and just so utterly sad. They will forever have in their thoughts the many people who died that day'.[1]*

Chapter 35

Jess continued. 'On that most dreadful day I would like to tell you the story of a young girl named Edie.

The sky was a brilliant blue the day death came to Thailand's Beaches. It was a day that changed Edie's life forever.

A family set off on Boxing Day morning for a day of Kayaking, a mother, her young daughter, and elder daughter, Edie, with her boyfriend. They hired two kayaks and set off from Ao Nang beach and spent a few minutes paddling across the sea.

They came to rest at a beautiful spot with limestone columns jutting out of the sea. It was so blissful. Edie took a picture of her mother and younger sister. The air suddenly felt different as though something was wrong. Looking out at sea in the very distance one could see a ridge, a wave, moving towards them which looked extremely unusual. It appeared something was terribly wrong. However, being a mile out to sea there would be no escape. A tremendous wave hit them all into a cliff face and Edie found herself tumbling under the water pushed by the force of the wave for what felt like minutes until she surfaced and saw her family all there alive.

Unfortunately another wave came and the same thing happened Edie was knocked against the rock face again and when she eventually surfaced they had been swept away. Her mother's body was later recovered, but her sister was never found and remained one of the many missing. Despite being badly injured, Edie managed to wait for the water levels to drop then crawled through a gap in the rocks. Cut and bleeding, she dragged herself away from the cliffs until she came to a beach. There she was reunited with her boyfriend, also injured but alive.

After hospital treatment she returned to the UK to a life of loss. Incredibly close to her mother and sister. Her mother was a strong passionate and loving mother while her sister was one of the most funny, loving and light-hearted people to be around. Now both were gone'.[1]*

Between stories Jess said. 'I think it is most important for those who are unaware to realise the devastation that can occur when a tsunami happens'. Quickly Jess cast an eye over her audience who all appear interested in the stories so far, Jess hoped this would continue.

'Louis was just 18 in Sri Lanka with his mother Zoe and brother Felix. This is his story':

"We were staying in an idyllic beach village called Unawatuna in Galle district. It took a matter of seconds for a wall of water about 5ft (1.52m) in height to start coming in. It was a kind of surge which reached the first floor of our hotel.

We tried to get people out. Miraculously, guests who had been in the room underneath us started popping up from the water.

One woman was trapped in her locked room because she could not find her key. She said the room filled up quickly with water and she took what she thought would be her last breath. Luckily she found the key and opened the door which then burst into pieces under the pressure.

Buildings were collapsing around us. We tried to pull out passing people trapped in the currents.

When the water finally subsided we made a run for higher ground and a temple that had become a make-shift safe refugee area. We set up camp in a hotel up on a hill. When it was safe to do so, we went back down to salvage anything we could. I remember seeing rooms full of mud and fish.

People came up to the temple with dead bodies. We carried one Italian woman with a suspected broken back through the debris to another hotel to get medical help. I met one guy who had been out surfing and was swept a few miles up the coast. He had to walk through all the death and destruction to find his family. Luckily he found them all.

One of the only positives to come out of it all was the humanity of it. It did not matter about your nationality or religion. Everyone checked on each other.

A few days later, once the road was clear, the High Commission sent coaches to take us back to a refuge centre in

Colombo. We were fed, watered, offered clothes and flights home but we chose not to go straight away. We wanted to stay to try and comprehend the reality of what had happened.

The main thing we felt was guilt. After seeing the devastation, we were lucky enough to leave, but many were left with nothing'.

Once in the UK, Louis put on an exhibition of the photos he'd managed to capture, Louis spoke about it at school and raised £3,500 to send back to the village.

"I gained a new found respect for the sea. I never realised its power. It hasn't put me off going into water, but I'm a lot more aware of what it can do".[1]*

Chapter 36

Jess took a final look around her audience and noticed there were a number actually in tears as they'd listened to some of the heart rending stories but sincerely felt that they needed to be told.

'One final mention' said Jess 'we've heard of the devastation of some families on holiday, but I would like to end with a story of an Indonesian family, a family who lived in the area so cruelly destructed'.

This story was reported, at the time, by a leading newspaper representative.

Indonesia: "We found them sifting through the putrid carpet of mud and debris covering the remains of their front room: a handsome young couple with three infant children determined to resurrect their lives when all they could see, smell and taste for miles around was death.

With sea drenching his cotton shirt and a filthy 'gag mask' covering his nose and mouth, the father, a 29 year old lorry driver named Sal Bini, repeatedly plunged his hands into the 3ft layer of mulch, searching for the simple possessions that might help his family start again.

I watched him unearth a plastic dinner plate, then the tin of chrome polish with which he would clean his truck before work each morning.

Later he dug out the plastic football he bought recently for his three-year old son Eri, and a tiny pair of tartan shoes belonging to his daughter Lela, six.

Each time Mr Bini made a find however small, he let out a low gasp of triumph.

Then, after scraping off as much dirt as he could, he carefully placed each item in a blue washing-up bowel which his wife Juliana, who carried their baby son Epi, in a sling, dragged to their salvage pile across the road.

The Bini family's village, Lampasi Engking, stood some two miles inland from the north-west coast of Sumatra. Yet, only a handful of its people survived.

The neighbours either side are missing presumed dead. So, too, are their best friends and many of their relatives.

On the day of the disaster Mr Bini was sitting at the breakfast table when he heard what sounded like the whoosh of a low-flying jet. Thinking a plane was about to crash nearby, dashed outside and saw hundreds of people fleeing in terror towards the hills.

Gathering up their children, he and his wife escaped to high ground two or three minutes before what he calls "the great black wave" came roaring in.

Minutes later, every last house on their road collapsed like matchwood. Yet although their rented two-bedroom home was built from timber with a corrugated roof, like all the rest, somehow only the front wall and part of the kitchen were washed away.

After five days Mr and Mrs Bini, now sheltering with their children in the garage where his lorry is parked, had dared to return to the teetering property, which threatened to collapse at any moment.

They worked defiantly and silently in tandem. Even when Mr Bini noticed a partially-buried corpse jutting out hideously from beneath the crumbling kitchen wall, the couple paused only briefly to bow their heads in respect before continuing to dig.

For in this vanished community, as in dozens more lost towns and villages along the rugged green Sumatran coastline dead bodies have become commonplace.

Wrapped in black or yellow plastic and shrouded in flies, they line the roads like so many recyclable council bin-bags, ready to be collected by police wagons and driven to one of the vast mass graves excavated around the provincial capital of Banda Aceh.

Now, as our immediate sense of compassion understandably begins to fade, the West's concerns must be for the living, too. Having heard reports of a £1billion international aid package, for many people in Aceh province, a vast tropical territory already torn by years of guerrilla warfare and where endemic diseases are rampant help will come too late.

True, the first cargo planes have started to arrive, at an airport which has been turned into a refugee camp.

The Red Cross and Medecins Sans Frontieres are here, and the thinly-stretched Indonesian authorities are showing admirable resourcefulness, flying in food, water and medical supplies.

There is, however, no sign in Banda Aceh of the huge concerted relief effort that had been promised and is so pressingly needed. It means there are woefully insufficient numbers of people and small aircraft to distribute the supplies to cut-off mainland towns, much less to the remote Indonesian archipelago. So tragically boxes of rice and bottles of purified water stand unopened.

While the waiting continued people are in danger of starving. Ordinarily, aid could be delivered by truck or flown in, but bridges have been torn down by the tsunami, leaving yawning chasms along the coast road.

At Meulaboh's tiny airport the runway is so badly damaged only helicopters and light planes can land.

Before the flood, 9,000 people lived there, but barely 3,000 cling to life in the few buildings still standing. Before this disaster zone, it was scarcely credible that a wave, however, mighty, could engulf a house three miles from the sea.

As we approached the coast, however, everything became unimaginable. For mile upon mile of flattened landscape, it was as though a giant boot had stamped down on the earth, squashing everything beneath it palm trees, houses, vehicles, cattle, people. Or rather almost everything, for bizarrely, here and there a building remained untouched. In one otherwise flattened road, a beautifully–designed pagoda-style house stood without so much as a brick dislodged, its pink-painted walls unblemished.

The sights were as surreal as they were macabre. Here lying in the road a headless cow, and a heavy lorry standing on end.

Beside a rice field, the body of a woman lay beside an upturned armchair as though she had just fallen out of it; other mud-covered corpses were almost indistinguishable from the fallen foliage.

At house number 11, in Ajun District, we helped police manoeuvre a wooden plank under a dead woman, whose presence had gone undetected for seven days. She lay in her kitchen beside a tin of chocolate waffles.

Further along the suffocating road, was the saddest image of all, that of a young mother who must have kept her arms wrapped tightly around her baby as the water closed in and killed them both.

All these wretched people are beyond our charity now, of course, but we can still help the living. The survivors like Sal and Juliana Bini and their three young children. Admirable uncomplaining people who have not asked for or received one penny of aid, and were visibly touched to learn that an appeal fund for victims like them had been set up by David's paper and that readers were keen to help.

Mr and Mrs Bini's hopes and aspirations were much the same as those of ordinary young British couples. Hard-working, self-reliant, and totally devoted to their children, they had been saving to buy a smart house of their own

Now their possessions can be fitted into two or three plastic washing-up bowels. Yet although they have lost everything, these indomitable Indonesians will never give up hope.

With their spirit and the help of generous readers they may one day attain the security and prosperity they were working towards before their dreams were so cruelly washed away".[1]*

Jess continued 'Many people were killed in the Thailand tsunami because they went down to the beach to view the receding ocean. A receding ocean may give you as little as a 5 minute warning to evacuate the area.

One final word on climate change' said Jess to her audience.

'The IPCC is a U.N. body of 195 member states that assesses the science related to the climate crisis.

The IPCC (Intergovernmental Panel on Climate Change) reports that humans are unequivocally driving global warming. Impacts are already seen from around the world with heatwaves to rising seas and extreme rain.

The world's leading climate scientists delivered their starkest warning yet about the deepening climate emergency, with some of the changes already set in motion thought to be 'irreversible' for centuries to come.

The climate panel warns that limiting global warming to close to 1.5°C or even 2°C above pre-industrial levels 'will be beyond reach' in the next two decades without immediate, rapid and large-scale reductions in greenhouse gas emissions.

The 1.5°C threshold is a crucial global target because beyond this level, so-called tipping points become more likely. Tipping points refer to an irreversible change in the climate system, locking in further global heating.

At 2°C of global warming, the report says heat extremes would often reach critical tolerance thresholds for agriculture and health.

U.N. Secretary-General, Antonio Guterres described the report as 'a code red for humanity'.

'The alarm bells are deafening, and the evidence is irrefutable: greenhouse gas emissions from fossil fuel burning and deforestation are choking our planet and putting billions of people at immediate risk' said Guterres.

Swedish climate activist Greta Thunberg said the report contained no real surprises. "We can still avoid the worst consequences, but not if we continue like today, and not without treating the crisis like a crisis".

The report shows that emissions of greenhouse gases from human activities are responsible for roughly 1.1°C of warming since 1850-1900, and find that averaged over the next 20 years global temperature is expected to reach or exceed 1.5°C of warming.

The U.N. climate panel says 'strong and sustained' reductions of carbon emissions and other greenhouse gases would limit climate change. Benefits such as improved air quality would come quickly, while it could take 20 to 30 years to see global temperatures stabilize.

The report makes it clear that it is not just about temperature. Climate change is bringing different changes in different regions – and all will increase with further global heating.

These changes include more intense rainfall and associated flooding, more intense drought in many regions, coastal areas to see continued sea level rise throughout the 21st century, the amplification of permafrost thawing, ocean acidification, among many others.

It follows a series of mind-bending extreme weather events worldwide. For instance, floods have wreaked havoc in Europe, China and India, toxic smoke plumes have blanketed Siberia and wild fires have burned out of control in the US, Canada, Greece and Turkey.

The IPCC had previously recognised that the necessary transition away from fossil fuels will be a huge undertaking that requires 'rapid, far-reaching and unprecedented changes' across all aspects of society.

It has underscored the point that limiting global warming to 1.5°C 'could go hand in hand with ensuring a more sustainable and equitable society' with clear benefits to both humans and natural ecosystems.

However, a U.N. analysis found that pledges made by countries around the world to curb greenhouse gas emissions were still 'very far' from the profound measures required to avoid the most devastating impacts of climate breakdown.'

Jess felt she had talked for far too long and truly hoped she'd managed to retain everyone's focus and attention.

'Thank you so much for listening', reiterated Jess 'I do hope this last part of the lecture has not been too distressing for some of you and, hopefully, helped to comprehend climate change. Thank you'.

Jess is amazed to hear an extremely loud round of applause, nodded her head in gratitude, smiled nervously and walked to her seat.

As soon as she was able, Miss Orchard managed to locate Jess surrounded by a group of attendees who'd thoroughly enjoyed her lecture. Most of them acknowledged their eyes had been truly opened on climate change.

Jess's headmistress intervened to guide her away from the group. 'I'm so proud of you Jess. What an excellent job speaking for such a long period about a most interesting topic'. 'Thank you' Jess responded. 'You must be exhausted'. 'Yes I do feel somewhat drained but I can now relax and listen to the other speakers' said Jess. Miss Orchard clutched her hand and whispered 'well done' as the next speaker took to the podium.

Jess thought it was about safety in the classroom but felt so emotionally exhausted did her level best not to nod off.

Thank goodness the speech was very short thought a grateful Jess also, at the same time, believed not very noble of her after she had taken so long to present her paper.

After the final speaker the Conference organiser appeared and thanked each participant and all attendees before everyone was dismissed for a welcome cup of tea and delightful cake.

PART THREE

Chapter 37

Claire spotted Jess as she seemed to tumble through her door. 'Gosh you look exhausted' exclaimed Claire 'did your talk go well?' 'I believe so but I am relieved it's over. Would you like to come in for a chat?' Jess questioned. 'No, drop your things then come upstairs to me and I will make you a welcome cup of tea'. 'Oh thank you, be with you in a minute' said a grateful Jess.

So relieved is Jess she can put her feet up, say a few words then listen to what Claire had to say.

It did not take them too long to have a quick discussion over tea as Jess is rather tired and really had no wish to go into too much detail about the Conference. However, they managed to arrange to have a walk through the meadow the next day, take a picnic, relax and enjoy the sun as Claire is on annual leave.

'That was such an enjoyable day out, thank you for suggesting it' said Jess. 'I think it did us both good' responded Claire 'especially for you after your exhausting day at the Conference'. 'Bye for now' said the girls as Claire disappeared upstairs to her flat and Jess to hers.

Jess noticed her telephone as it flashed with a message. Oh is it Mike calling at long last was her initial thought. No it was Grace, her dear mother who asked Jess to call her. 'Hi Mum so sorry I hadn't got round to ring you yet'. It's ok dear' was her mother's reply 'I'm sure you were shattered after the conference'. Jess briefly brought her mother up to date with her conference presentation on climate change then asked after everyone.

'Well that's one reason I needed to speak to you' retorted Grace. 'I'm worried about Holly because I believe her boyfriend Chris is a drug addict, well not exactly an addict but there is definitely something odd about him'. 'What gave you that impression Mum? 'Initially, I thought Chris a pleasant, happy young man but I've witnessed him in a different light which I'd failed to notice before.

Holly brought him for dinner when I had the opportunity to observe him more closely. I saw his eyes were blood-shot, his skin tone did not look so good and he appeared extremely tired as if all he wanted to do was sleep. Dad mentioned it to me later so he had noticed too.

This had me rather worried for Holly as she would talk about him somewhat which led me to believe that their friendship could become quite serious.

I questioned Holly later but she hadn't detected anything. She'd not seen too much of him of late due to her busy work schedule and the show she'd agreed to take part in'.

'Mum you need to get to the bottom of this just in case Chris is an addict. Have another discreet word with Holly, that's if she's keen to continue with him. It's necessary for her to have a diplomatic and sensitive word with Chris to try to find what's possibly troubling him as soon as possible. Then perhaps we can have a further discussion as to what to do. Oh Mum what a mess if he is, and poor Holly as she does seem rather keen on him'.

'I'm glad I've mentioned my fears to you. I'm worried Dad would have little patience if he found out if this happened to be true'. Their conversation ended with love and hugs and words of 'try not to worry'.

Oh my goodness pondered Jess, what an absolute worry for Mum with Holly so keen on Chris. If only Mike would ring he would know what to do. Put him out of you mind girl Jess pondered a second time. Perhaps she could discuss with Josie when next they met. In the meantime Jess realised she must get her head around this possible problem, do some research into drug addiction as really she had no clue as to what to do.

The conversation with her mother had led Jess to think of Mike. Despite her thoughts he'd currently been tied up with another difficult case with his assistant Dan. They were exceedingly busy doing their utmost to identify a human trafficking gang.

Information had come about after a desperate father had contacted Police Headquarters to explain his fears as to what might have happened to his daughter and her friend.

In a desperate state the father named, Ben Bartlett had alerted Police HQ about Sally, his daughter. He'd explained he was divorced from Sally's mother who had remarried and Sally lived with them. Ben was amicable with his ex-wife and partner and went to visit his daughter at their home. Whilst there, they all tried to persuade him to sign a parental document for Sally to visit Paris. Ben was most reluctant to do such a thing as she was not yet 18. Emotionally overpowered by the three of them he gave in and eventually signed. However, this was on condition that she telephoned her father each and every evening which Sally promised to do. Ben wished her well with the proviso to avoid certain parts of Paris. Sally was overcome with excitement and aimed to travel with her friend Millie over the weekend.

Ben did not feel too happy as he left, but gave Sally a hug and kiss, together with words of caution to be very careful and not to forget to call him.

An excited Sally called her father on arrival in Paris and said she would call again that evening.

Now at Police HQ Ben was rather distraught with worry as he'd had no word from Sally for three days. He went on to explain that he'd tried her mobile phone several times but nothing and now frantic for her safety.

Ben further stated that before going to Police HQ he'd undergone a little research about safety of young girls in Paris. After which he decided to travel alone to the capital to do his utmost to find her.

While he waited for a taxi, he'd witnessed a handsome rather respectable looking young man as he sidled up to a couple of pretty young ladies as they too waited for a taxi. Ben overheard him offer, in an extremely subtle tone, to share the taxi with them.

Ben, about to get into a taxi himself for his hotel, had stood directly next to the young man and the two girls. He then requested that his driver follow the taxi in front as it drew away with the occupants. The driver ahead eventually came to a halt outside, what looked very much like a block of flats. Ben explained to his driver that he needed to hop out and for him to wait.

Ben did just that and waited close by to do his best to hear what might be said, but also discreet enough to not cause concern. He heard the young man when he said 'there's a dance tomorrow night at the (Ben could not hear where) would you like to come?' One of the two girls appeared more enthusiastic than the other and replied 'yes we'd love to'. Ben overheard him as he spoke and said 'Ok, I'll pick you up at 7pm then'. The young man appeared to look the building up and down pulled out a notebook as if to note the address. Ben then returned to his taxi with the thought that this could be entirely innocent.

However, Ben had gone to the address, his daughter Sally had given him, a few hours before and found the doors locked with no response to his knock. He'd managed to get inside and it appeared that the girls had left in a hurry and still there was no message from Sally. By this time he was extremely upset, worried and angry. All of these emotions were hammering through his head but he told himself to stay calm and would definitely be around at 7pm the following evening, the time the two girls were due to be picked up.

At around 7pm the next day Ben hired a taxi and asked his driver to stop and let him out opposite to the flats he wished to watch and asked the driver to wait.

The same young man Ben witnessed entered the flats and came out at the front entrance alone. He beckoned to two others and Ben observed three men go back inside the premises. He could only guess that the two girls had changed their minds about going to the dance. Probably egged on by the girl who the day before had appeared less keen.

He continued to wait and before long, the three men appeared to force the two girls into their car. It seemed obvious to Ben the girls now showed some reluctance to go with these individuals but, nevertheless, they were bundled into the car.

Ben had to explain to his driver, who he hoped was a decent and caring human being, why he wished him to follow them. As the car pulled away Ben's driver seemed happy to follow. The car ultimately pulled up alongside rather salubrious premises, a three story property in an expensive area of the city. He witnessed the two girls as they were led, or rather pushed from behind, up some steps into the building.

Perhaps this was not as innocent as Ben had first thought so, therefore, asked his driver to take him to the airport. Ben felt this could be too big a deal for him to handle alone and would definitely require help.

Mike, together with his assistant Dan, had been alerted by a member of their team. Ben had made his statement to this team member who felt that Mike should be notified. Both Mike and Dan listened with great interest and concern to his story. Mike did not wish to alarm Ben more at this stage but felt pretty certain this was very likely to be a foreign trafficking gang that HQ had heard so much about.

'We'll do our utmost to find your daughter and her friend explained Mike. I suggest you get yourself a cup of tea while we have a brief meeting I will then inform you of our plan of action'. 'Ok' said Ben 'Thankyou' left the room and closed the door behind him.

Mike held an urgent meeting with Dan and several CID members to plan their undercover pursuit of this, most probable, perilous foreign activity. In total agreement it is concluded this is a matter of extreme urgency. If a trafficking gang are holding Sally and her friend, it is imperative they travel to Paris post haste. These two girls must be saved and, hopefully, bring whoever's responsible to justice. From the information Ben had passed to HQ, Mike is more than certain the girls had fallen into the hands of a scrupulous human trafficking gang.

Before Ben is informed of their intention, Mike ordered a team member to organise their immediate transport to Paris. He has a strong suspicious gut feeling there is no time to lose.

Ben is brought into the small conference room where Mike explained in as much detail as possible what he and his team intend to do. For him to rest assured that they all are extremely well trained for this type of operation.

Overwhelmed with gratitude, Ben asked if he could accompany them. Mike responded 'by all means you may travel with us but then I must ask you to stay well clear, find something to occupy yourself. I have your mobile number and will contact you as and when we possibly could have some information. Ok, clear?' 'Yes, thank you so much' agreed a most appreciative Ben.

Within a fairly short time the team are in Paris and two members observe the property from a distance, the address given to them by Ben. Pete and Alan, part of the CID team, relay their findings to Mike and Dan who are at the Paris Police HQ. Here, with the Paris police, they do their best to check out possible foreign traffickers.

Pete spoke quietly through his intercom that they had witnessed four males as they entered the property but no sign of any young girls.

Mike acknowledged Pete's information and told him to continue to watch and if anyone should leave to follow and for him and Joe to do their best to befriend them.

No sooner had Mike made this suggestion when Pete hurriedly said 'two men are about to leave now'. 'Ok, good luck Pete, keep in touch'.

The two men are followed in their car by Pete and Joe until they pull alongside a Public House and drove to the car park at the rear.

Pete, of course, entered the Pub separately from Joe walked to the Bar and ordered a drink. The two men are stood alongside and he discreetly made a mental note of both. Pete rather surprised that both of these men actually look reasonably respectful characters. However he noticed the accent was definitely not British.

It did not take long for Pete to open up a conversation with these two individuals. He, at the same time, ascertained that they were on the prowl for male clients willing to pay a substantial sum of money for a lovely young girl. Pete was exceedingly shrewd in the way he got the men to reveal their activity and to lead them on that he was on the look-out for a girl himself to seduce.

Pete, as he stood beside the two men, had their backs to Joe, who had sauntered into the Pub a few minutes after Pete. Joe, with his eye on the two men at the Bar surreptitiously picked up his phone to update Mike who suggested Joe did his best to muscle in on their conversation. To somehow do their level best to be invited back to their premises. Mike continued that he and Dan would not be too far away when the time was right to call him. 'Ok' whispered Joe.

Joe then proceeded to the opposite end of the Bar from Pete and the two men. As he ordered a drink, Pete turned and in a rather loud voice said 'hi Joe, haven't seen you in a while, how're things?' 'Good to see you Pete' with a shrug of his shoulders.

'Come and join us' said Pete. 'Oh it's ok' said Joe in a nonchalant manner 'you're with two other mates'. 'I've only met them here in the Pub, come on, come and join us be great to catch up'. Joe sauntered over. Pete said 'meet my two new mates, Ivan and Ches' and pointed to which one was which. With a nod to each Joe shook their hands.

'He's ok' Pete pointed out to Ivan and Ches 'much like me always on the look-out for a pretty girl. 'If you're sure, that's ok then' Ivan responded. 'So what're you prepared to pay for a pretty young girl,' Pete replied 'depends what you have to offer'.

Joe looked on in a gleeful manner with eyes raised in the hope the men might think he was most excited with this proposition.

'What if the girls you have don't take a shine to me, or us now,' Pete remarked. 'Oh they will like you, you can be assured'.

'Well I don't know about you Joe but I'd like to see what I'm paying for first' said Pete. 'Yea, me too' agreed Joe.

The two men had obviously explained in detail to Pete, before Joe joined in, what they'd done to the girls to get them to do exactly what was demanded of them. Without so much of a flinch from Pete, although he felt pretty sick inside at the thought. With Pete's extremely good acting skills Ivan and

Ches felt reassured they would have no problem and could really trust him. This went for Joe too as he clearly was a great friend of Pete's.

After a short while Joe excused himself to go to the gents. He quickly relayed an update message to Mike when he heard the door open and immediately tucked away his 'phone and feigned tidying his trousers. It was Ivan 'just double checking you mate'. 'Of course, no problem' said Joe and walked back to the Bar'

Ivan returned to the Bar and said 'why don't you follow us back to our place. I think it would be better Pete if I come with you in your car and Ches can take Joe. We'll get you a very nice girl each for a price'. 'Ok, that sounds good to me' replied Pete 'ok with you Joe?' 'Yea great' Joe nodded.

With the information Joe had passed on. Mike and Dan made a quick decision to raid the property before they got there.

Within a few minutes they arrived at the premises in question, together with two CID Paris members. The four of them ascend the steps to the door it is, of course, locked but with their trained skills managed to get it open.

There are three floors to this property. It's eerily quiet with no sign of anyone on the first floor which looked more like an office with a Board Table and several computers.

The second floor is quite horrific as they find several girls in a dazed state in different rooms. One girl is tied to the bed and looked almost unconscious. Immediately Mike untied her and did his best to speak to her to no avail. Dan did his best to ask the name of each girl located in different rooms. One even tried to put her arms around him, he discreetly removed them.

Mike, Dan and the two Police Officers cannot imagine what drug these awful people had given these girls to behave like zombies. One or two of them look as though they'd been beaten as bruises are clear to see.

Dan explained to Mike that he'd got a few names from the girls but no one named Sally, Ben's daughter. However he'd managed to get a little sense from, he hoped was, her friend Millie, who mumbled something about sold to someone.

Now beside himself with anger Mike heard Pete, Joe and the two men as they arrived. Ivan whizzed up the stairs as he'd thought one of the girls must have unlocked the door. He was taken aback to see Mike, Dan and two Police Officers who stepped forward immediately and handcuffed Ivan. As Ches tried to escape, Pete and Joe forced him inside and he too was handcuffed. Ivan then spat at Pete with some foreign expletive. Ches, on the other hand, tried his best to thump Joe without success.

'Ok' said Mike 'what have you done with a girl named Sally?' Both Ivan and Ches shrugged their shoulders. 'If you know what's good for you, you'd better tell us. We have information that you've sold her on to some ruthless or heartless person, who is he and where is he?'

Still reluctant to give Mike the information, the Paris police officers forced both men into a chair and jabbered away in French to them. Both men began to look rather nervous, Ches more so than Ivan who then gave an address to the Police Officer. Ivan scowled at Ches ferociously as he gave this information. There were evidently more than these two working together in this hideous crime. At this stage, however, they were adamant not to give any names to the police. The French police had assured Ivan and his accomplice that they would indeed find them.

Mike spoke in French to the more senior Police Officer with a request to get these girls released immediately to attend hospital to be checked over and cared for. The Officer made an order for a police van to take the two scoundrels into custody as he and his team member would be on their way to find this supposed unsavoury character.

While they waited for the two men to be taken into custody, Mike made contact with Ben and asked him to join them. Warned him not to be too optimistic but there was a possibility they may find his daughter Sally.

Ben met Mike and his team outside the property and witnessed the Police Van with two of the culprits inside

Mike, Dan, Pete and Joe followed the French police to the address where this supposed callous person lived. They pulled up outside a large gated establishment with two security guards outside.

Police Officer Thierrie showed his details at the gates which were then opened. He then beckoned everyone to follow.

The building was very majestic, like a palace with guards and people milling around. Thierrie marched through the large hallway, approached by a Butler and demanded to see his boss. He was told he was busy. Thierrie commanded to see him now, this very minute.

The so called Butler had no choice but to take Thierrie and the team through to his boss. There he was sitting in splendour as they witnessed a clearly frightened girl before him. Mike turned and looked at Ben who nodded as tears trickled down his cheeks. This was his daughter Sally.

After much questioning, the boss of this so called establishment was marched off by the French Police Officers. He'd obviously paid a lot of money for this English girl to this foreign team of despicable individuals.

Sally had been drugged to a certain extent and seemed unaware of what was happening around her. She did not appear to recognise her father at once but as he sat her down and spoke to her softly and gently she understood and put her arms around him and sobbed uncontrollably.

Mike and Dan then found Millie at the local hospital, who was not in a good way. However, they flew back to Heathrow together and deposited Millie to her home. Ben could not thank Mike and his team enough for what they had undergone and achieved success. They'd located Sally and Millie and ensured that the other girls taken by these ruthless men would be cared for and returned to their homes too.[1]*

Chapter 38

In the meantime Jess with concern of her mother's conversation popped upstairs for a chat with Claire to take her mind off her despair.

'Hi Claire thought I'd pop in for a few minutes if that's ok with you'. 'Of course Jess so good to see you we can have a catch up, come in'.

Claire quickly put on the kettle for them to sit down with a welcome cup of tea. Jess did not mention her concern that clouded her mind over her mother's conversation about Chris but listened intently to her flat mate which definitely helped to take her mind off the situation.

'Remember Jess when I mentioned to you some time ago I felt a romantic attraction to Jim who I worked fairly closely with? Well eventually I realised his only interest in me was as a studious, helpful and intelligent colleague and obviously going no further than a team player'.

'Oh that was sad for you Claire as I remember you were rather infatuated with Jim'. 'Yes, but I've definitely moved on from him now Jess. I've wanted to share this with you but recently we've been like 'ships passing in the night''.

Now focussed on what Claire was about to disclose 'can't wait to hear' said Jess with a tinge of excitement.

Claire began with how she had first encountered Adrian, a Paediatric Surgeon. Jim had held a drinks party at his home and, of course she had been invited. Claire had noticed, at the time, there did not appear to be any sign of a girlfriend with Jim just a group of doctors, nurses and a few senior administrative staff.

Adrian offered her a drink and remained with her the whole evening as they enjoyed their chat together. Claire continued that it became rather obvious that he had taken a shine to her and, of course, Claire thought him handsome, intelligent and quick witted.

'Since that night, we've had a couple of dates together and get on really well and I have grown rather fond of him' Claire retorted. 'So watch this space Jess'.

'Wow Claire, that's wonderful news' Jess exclaimed.

'That's enough about my life, time you updated me with what's been happening with you recently Jess'.

'No a great deal' responded Jess rather flatly. 'My class of children remain delightful and I've heard nothing from Mike now for some time so I reluctantly believe I too should move on from him'

'I'm so sorry to hear that Jess but somehow I have a feeling you are not lost to him'. With a weak smile Jess thanked Claire for the welcome cup-of tea and reiterated just how delighted she was with her news then made her way back to her own flat.

Jess welcomed her class of children back to school with words of just how much she'd missed them and hoped they'd had a wonderful time.

The children were happy to have a rather relaxed morning with their first day back. Everyone chatted excitedly with their teacher as they cheerfully managed to reveal some of their compelling stories of their long holiday from school. .

Also Jess needed confirmation from them that they had indeed looked at their exercise books occasionally to help remember what they had learned last term. How very pleased Jess was to hear that most of the children had retained a lot of what she'd done her upmost to teach.

Over the weekend before the start of the new term, instead of having fun which really what Jess would have preferred, she'd spent the time drawing a map of Europe for her class. She believed it important for them to know about the countries that surround the United Kingdom. Jess chose the nearest eleven countries to the UK and made a plan to look a little like a puzzle. She drew the shape of each country but left the name blank for the children to fill in and, hopefully, help them to learn and retain the name of each country.

It had taken Jess rather a long while to complete this task, although she was pretty good with her artwork.

Jess greeted the children after their lunch break and explained that they were about to learn about the countries in

Europe and their capital cities. She distributed a paper with her artwork to each of them which displayed the shape of each country.

'We must try to do our best to make this fun' Jess continued as she explained the paper in front of them with an outline image of the various countries which surround the United Kingdom.

'You can see that I have drawn these countries on my Board in various different colours. When I tell you the country, write down the name. You will see from the shape which country is which'. They all seemed quite happy with this so Jess proceeded.

Jess explained that there are 195 countries in the world which are far too many for them to learn today so they will start with just eleven closest to our own.

'We'll start with the United Kingdom, we all know the shape of our own country don't we?' 'Yes' most of the children chanted. 'So just write down UK and who can tell me the capital of our country?' Nearly every hand shot up, Jess thought it pretty good most children at least knew the capital of their own country. 'Ok so right down London underneath UK'. 'Well that wasn't difficult was it?'

Jess helped the children with the other 10 countries. She pointed out on her blackboard the various countries and started with the ones nearest to the UK. As with the UK and London as its capital the children were asked to write the capital city underneath the name of each country, as they had been listed on the blackboard as follows:

· France : Paris, Germany : Berlin, Brussels : Belgium, Netherlands : Amsterdam, Denmark : Copenhagen, Finland : Helsinki, Sweden : Stockholm, Norway : Oslo, Switzerland : Bern, Spain : Madrid, and Portugal : Lisbon.

'When you've finished writing the names down, I would like you to shade the countries in the colour I've displayed on the board' said Jess.

It is all peaceful and quiet as the children get on with the task in hand which enabled Jess to prepare for their next lesson.

After some minutes a hand shot up 'finished' then another and another. Jess then decided to walk around the classroom to check if anyone had struggled. No, they'd all done very well even Tommy who seemed a lot better and happier since Jess had done her best to take a special interest in him since the loss of his mother.

However, she did have to correct Billy and Emma who'd put a country in the wrong position, which would mean that two countries are incorrectly named. Jess was very pleased with all of them, how very proud she was and hoped they would learn the countries and their capitals.

'So children I would like you to take your drawings of the countries home and please look at them from time to time'. The children wanted so much to please their teacher so most children nod and said they would.

Chapter 39

Jess's thoughts were 'live for the moment' and decided to go for a brisk walk. As she passed her school, all was quiet and serene when she bumped into John Barlow, the Deputy Head, also out on a walk after he'd done some work at the school premises.

'Hello Jess what's brought you this way, not missing school are you?' he jests. 'Hi John, how nice to see you I'm out for a bit of exercise at the moment'. 'I'm off to the Café for coffee would you like to join me?' 'Ok John, yes that would be nice'. Jess guessed John would be about 10 years or so her senior but knew little of his personal life.

Over coffee they had a very friendly conversation between them when Jess felt confident enough to question John a little about his life away from school. She was most surprised when he revealed he had never married, although he'd had a serious relationship some years ago but, unfortunately, it hadn't worked out. 'Oh I'm so sorry to hear that' said Jess. John continued that he'd, therefore, thrown his energies into school life.

'Do you intend to remain a bachelor forever?' responded a bold Jess. 'No, if I'm ever in the right place at the right time, you never know' was his reply.

Jess mentioned a little about what she'd done over the school holiday, her trip to Ibiza and the Conference but not in any great detail. She didn't mention Mike, of course, whom she was desperate to push out of her head but nevertheless he remained deep at the back of her mind.

John was very friendly, almost too much so Jess felt. The last thing she wanted was for him to ask her out. No way did she wish to get involved with a member of her school staff.

The way he looked and spoke to her Jess knew somehow she must bring this brief meet up to a close. 'It's been so good to catch up with you John with a very pleasant chat together but I must be off now, so much to do'.

John rose from his chair took her hand in his 'so good to see you Jess, thank you for coming, I really enjoyed our conversation'. 'Oh no need, I enjoyed it too' said Jess 'really look forward to seeing you back at school next term John' squeezed his hand and left.

Phew that was close Jess thought as she ambled back home.

Jess saw her landline light as it flashed with a message. 'Mm she thought I wonder who that might be is, deep down she continued to hope and wonder if it might be Mike.

'Hi Jess, Josie hear do hope all is well. I would like to meet up with you, please give me a call to let me know when you're free, bye'.

Jess called Josie right away and after a brief chat arranged to meet the next day which happened to be Saturday and a day off for Josie.

Jess greeted her at the door with a cheerful hello and hug and off they went together in Josie's car. 'Shall we go to that country pub by the river we came across before?' Josie asked. 'That would be wonderful' said Jess 'but it's just nice for us to be together at last'.

As they motored along 'I want to update you Jess, my friendship with Peter fizzled out yet again so definitely not meant to be together for the long haul'. 'I'm not at all surprised' Jess responded. 'I really liked Peter but I was never too sure that you two were a match'. 'You're always right Jess'.

'Anyway, Jeff and I have become an item and I am so exceedingly happy, as I believe he is too'. 'Oh gosh Josie that's great, everyone appears to have managed to get their lives together with the right person at long last'.

Jess did solemnly think to herself, except her, but continued briefly as she mentioned to Josie her flat mate Claire's good news too.

Josie needed to talk to Jess about Mike. The weather fortunately was a nice pleasant sunny day so she suggested that they take their lunch outside where they sat by the river and also rather quiet.

After a brief catch up chat Josie began with the story that had been relayed to her by Mike's friend Jeff, now her boyfriend.

'Jess I think it only fair that I tell you a little about Mike'. Jess looked a little alarmed at this statement because her dear friend Josie looked quite serious. She went on and described that Mike and Jeff had been great friends for a very long time although they both worked at Police Headquarters in completely different areas, Mike in forensics and Jeff mostly with laboratory work. They, had in fact, known one another from their school days and were firm friends

Josie explained 'Jeff and I popped out for lunch together the other day and he felt it was time to tell me a little of Mike's background, principally because I was a true friend of you, Jess. Jeff didn't want you to be hurt or disappointed when Mike, at times, behaved in a haphazard-way'. By this time Jess began to feel her stomach churn, what would be revealed next as she had felt a bond between herself and Mike some time back?

Josie must continue although she could feel her best friend's anxiety. 'Jeff had gone on to mention the time when Mike had been tremendously happy with his long term girlfriend, Lucy. They were engaged to be married and, in a nutshell, Lucy became very ill and, over a short period, lost her fight for life. After Lucy passed away Mike became withdrawn and threw himself into his work and was determined never to have a serious relationship with a girl again. It was Jeff who'd persuaded him to go out as a foursome that night when we all went out for dinner.

Mike, if you remember, put on a good show but Jeff felt that he could have led you on as he'd tried so hard to be brave which quite possibly may have misled you.

Anyway Jeff said that he'd seen Mike happy for the first time in a long while after we'd been out together. However, after some thought, Jeff became worried that Mike might be inconsistent with his contact with you and felt the time was now right for you to know a little of Mike's background to try to understand him better'.

Josie took Jess's hand as she looked close to tears. 'Thank you for the explanation' said Jess as a tear trickled down her cheek. Josie then said 'if and when Mike does contact you, it would probably be better if you kept what I've told you to yourself to shield Jeff as he didn't have Mike's permission to reveal this'. 'Of course' she responded 'but I'm so pleased you've told me as I can now see Mike in a different light and how much he must have truly suffered at the tragic loss of his girlfriend.

Thank you again Josie for sharing this with me and, of course, I will keep it to myself and hope, one day, Mike will confide in me that's if he does ever again make contact. Please thank Jeff for me that he allowed you to bring this sad episode to my attention'.

The girls do their best not to dwell on the matter and force themselves to talk about other less serious topics

Alone at last Jess was overcome with emotion as she sat and mulled over the information Josie had conveyed to her. Without doubt Jess now completely understood how Mike had appeared to blow hot and cold with regard to their irregular meetings. Jess hoped against hope that Mike would contact her sometime and pondered deeply how she could help him move on.

Jess did not reveal to Josie her mother's concern with regard to Holly's supposed boyfriend Chris. For one reason she did not know how serious her sister's relationship was with him. It didn't stop her worrying about the situation though and, of course, with no real clue as to how to help.

Also Jess had not heard from Holly recently which she had expected to if only to hear about the show she may have a singing part in.

Chapter 40

Mike had not made contact with Jess for some time now. He had at long last come to the conclusion, with help from his close mate Jeff, that he cannot mourn his dear adorable Lucy for the rest of his life.

He'd clung to Lucy's memory for an indeterminate time. Perhaps he was able to draw strength from this, who knows, but it had prevented him from getting on and living life and quite possibly now the loss of Jess with whom he'd felt an attachment, albeit with his heart still entwined with Lucy's.

At long last, with the added intervention of Jeff, he'd reached a decision to do his best to move on. He hoped against hope that Jess was not already lost to him but, whatever, he must bury Lucy but deep in his heart where she would forever hold a special place.

Over many months Mike lost himself completely as he concentrated solely on his work. This enabled him to think of nothing else, not either on Lucy or Jess. Alas this, he realised, was a red herring and must sooner or later face reality and scolded himself in no uncertain terms. To face up to life whatever may be in store even with the possibility of the loss of Jess, due to his lack of contact and communication which he sincerely hoped would not be so.

More than a couple of weeks had passed since Josie had opened up to Jess about Mike's past life when, at long last, he plucked up courage to call her. He truly felt he must not mess this girl's life up any further which he proposed to himself before he made the call. Of course, on the other hand, this darling girl may have washed her hands of him entirely.

Mike was well aware that he may justifiably be rejected but swallowed his pride and braved himself to make the call one Friday evening.

'Hello' said Jess in answer to the ring of the telephone. Oh my goodness Mike, quick as a flash the thought raced through her head.

'Hello Jess, look I have no excuse for my lack of contact but it would make me most happy if you would agree to meet up with me again'. Jess's immediate thought was what a relief to hear from him. At long last I could possibly mention Mum's worry to him about Chris. However, she remained cool and calm as she responded.

'Mmmmmm' was her immediate response as, of course, she must keep to herself the knowledge she'd received from Josie about Mike's past life. After a slight pause said 'ok Mike perhaps it might be a better idea if you popped round to my flat, say, tomorrow afternoon for a cup of tea when we can have a chat together'.

Jess thought maybe that was the best idea to suggest, under the circumstances. 'Say about 2.30' suggested Jess.

'Ok fine' Mike responded. 'Really look forward to seeing you Jess, bye for now'. 'Bye' said Jess and replaced the receiver. Gosh Jess's first thought was she probably sounded rather distant which was the worried thought that raced through her mind. However, perhaps that's how she should have reacted through his lack of contact she consoled herself. No way did she wish to reveal what she'd learned from Josie about his loss of Lucy so Jess comforted and confirmed to herself that her immediate response was probably the correct way to respond.

Jess busied herself in preparation for Mike's visit and made a cake. Just a simple Victoria Sponge but it did look rather delicious. The least she could do was to offer tea and cake as she was uncertain as to how the visit would go.

Mike turned up on the dot at 2.30pm. Jess greeted him kindly and ushered him through her flat to the spacious sitting room and guided him to the large sofa.. Jess decided not sit alongside him but sat in a chair opposite in order for them to face each other. For the first time Jess felt aware of his awkwardness so immediately did her best to put him at ease.

Briefly they touched on what each of them had been doing during their isolation. 'Would you like a cup of tea and a piece of my homemade cake' Jess suggested. 'That would be nice, thank you'.

Mike did not know whether to follow Jess into the kitchen or stay put. He decided not to and remained seated.

Jess quickly returned with a tray and passed Mike his tea with a slice of cake. 'Thank you Jess this looks delicious' he remarked. 'Try it first' Jess responded and sat down beside him on the sofa.

After a couple of mouthfuls 'delicious it is' he reiterated when Jess noticed he began to relax. Thank goodness she thought and decided to ask Mike a little about his job.

'Do you really want to talk about my job' he asked. 'Yes, I would, I know nothing about police work and I'd like to be educated'. 'So what would you like to know?' 'Basically qualifications one would require to do your job so why don't you start from the beginning'.

'Ok' said Mike 'I intend to make this brief as I don't wish to talk about this in depth. Mike continued that he was first and foremost a trained Police Officer and really wanted to move on to become a Crime Investigator who, not only, are highly regarded by the police but that was his initial aim.

A degree is required in Chemistry or Biology and Mike relayed that his degree was in Chemistry. Basically we collect and document physical evidence, take photographs and prepare diagrams of crime scenes and write up investigation reports. We deal with drug trafficking, national security and terrorism. Myself, or my team are on call day or night as crimes happen at any time without notice.

'Do you carry guns?' Jess enquired. Mike's brief response to her question was 'Yes, does that satisfy you Miss Aries? Jess chuckled with a yes response.

The two of them were now far more relaxed with one another but Mike desired to know what Jess too had been doing during their absence.

Jess reminded and enlightened him about her climate change passion as she was aware this concern was not one of Mike's interests. In between the seriousness of their updated conversation, Jess could feel the warmth between them.

Time, however, was getting on 'would you like to stay for dinner?' Jess enquired. Mike reached for her hand at this question and replied 'yes I would like that very much on one condition that you allow me into the kitchen to help'. Jess laughed at his suggestion 'if you insist'.

Jess informed Mike that she did not wish them to spend too much time in the kitchen and would cook something simple and hoped he wasn't going to expect a gourmet meal.

'If you would top and tail these green beans Mike while I prepare the chicken'. They laughed and joked together and in a very short while seasoned chicken with green beans and a few oven chips were ready to eat. With a glass of wine it did look rather tasty.

Everything between them was so much better, more so than Jess had ever experienced with Mike before. It was so obvious that Mike too was thoroughly enjoying himself. There was no pudding so another piece of Victoria Sponge was placed before him.

The empty dishes were quickly placed in the dishwasher before settling down to relax once more.

Mike now had his arm around Jess and thanked her most profusely for the delightful meal and enchanting company.

Now both very relaxed and loosened up Jess wished to bring up Chris, her sister Holly's boyfriend, and the telephone call she'd received recently from her mother. It had worried Jess but half of her wanted this day to be about the two of them not to bring up something to disturb their togetherness. So decided now, most definitely, was not the right time after their most enjoyable afternoon and evening together.

Sat comfortably with a cup of coffee after their meal, Mike took both of Jess's hands in his, looked deep into her eyes 'I would like us to see much more of each other, would you like that too?'. Mike sensed Jess was open to hear these words from him and was more than happy when she replied. 'Yes, Mike I would love to see more of you but much more frequently not just now and then as before'.

'I'd very much like to take you out for the day tomorrow, is that soon enough?' he suggested. 'Oh my goodness, I would love that' Jess agreed. So arrangements were made to travel to Brighton for the day and he would pick her up the next morning, a Sunday, at 1000am.

It was now time for him to depart as it was almost 1030pm. The time had flown by with so much talked about. Mike pulled Jess up from the sofa and with his arm around her shoulder walked to the door. He cupped her chin in his hand and kissed her tenderly goodnight. 'Goodnight Mike, thank you for coming I've really enjoyed your company'. With a truly wonderful smile and a quick peck on her cheek, he left with, see you in the morning.

Jess closed the door with a delightful feeling in her heart and the excitement of tomorrow to look forward to. However she still had not mentioned the Chris concern which still bothered her.

Chapter 41

It was bright and fairly early on Sunday morning when Mike appeared. Jess opened the door already to leave. Mike actually greeted her with a peck on the cheek.

Oh it was so nice to see him in this lovely frame of mind thought Jess as they ambled to his car. Jess sat back in the car and relaxed for their journey to Brighton. 'I'll teach you to drive one day' said Mike. 'I can't wait' she responded with a thank you.

They chatted all the way about work and life in general, how Mike hoped they could eventually become more than mere friends. Jess thoroughly enjoyed these words as they flowed from his lips as she'd felt a bond with him since they'd first met. She responded that she hoped so too.

After their most comfortable journey 'let's have a quick lunch' Mike suggested and soon found a smart Café. After a quick snack for lunch they left and moved on. Now in the centre of Brighton Mike found a suitable parking space and off they walked hand in hand.

The stunning summer afternoon with the salt laden air and squawking seagulls overhead against an unbroken sky was rather heavenly with this lovely man by her side thought a very happy Jess.

As they walked down the street with eyes only for each other, they noticed the elegant white painted lined Regency type houses with their iron railings as they passed by.

Together they decided to visit the Brighton Pavilion as both were interested in history and architecture and it was just a short distance away.

It was rather ecstatic for the two of them just to be together as they wandered through this exciting place full of history.

'Wow' said Mike 'I really didn't know much about the history of the Brighton Pavilion that it was built in 1787 by an Architect named Henry Holland'. 'I didn't know that either' Jess responded.

Both are completely absorbed by the information before them. George IV, then the Prince of Wales, hired Henry Holland to transform his Brighton Lodging House into a modest Villa known then as the Marine Pavilion, which became George's home when in Brighton.

Jess turned to Mike with the words 'I guess his Lodging House was more of a palace by our standards made into a modest Villa which most definitely would have been a palace'. 'You bet' said Mike with an expression like, ok for some.

As they continued through the great hall still hand in hand they came across a scroll of writing. In 1811 George was sworn in as Prince Regent as his father George III was at that time incapable of acting as Monarch.

George in 1815 then commissioned Architect John Nash to transform the modest Villa into the magnificent oriental palace that we see today.

In the Music Room are six colossal porcelain Chinese Pagodas, probably made for George in China in the early 19th century. The exotic Palace was covered in Chandeliers, beautiful palm trees and amazing paintings. There was a colourful, eye-catching Banqueting Hall and the Kitchen a taste of the orient.

George became King in 1820 but made only two further visits in 1824 and 1827.

At the end of their visit a notice revealed that in WW1 the Pavilion was transformed into a Hospital.

Jess squeezed Mike's hand 'well that was incredibly mind-blowing' she said   Mike looked at Jess with a loving smile 'yes, that was really something'.

They made their way out of the Pavilion and took a walk in the glorious sunshine along the promenade as the beach is rather pebbly. Oh this is so wonderful thought Jess as both laughed and chatted in a way one could imagine them as true lovers.

Eventually a rather nice restaurant is found so both decide to have an early supper before their journey home. Mike and Jess discussed their day over supper. The bond between them had grown stronger and both were so happy together in this instant.

Jess was rather desperate to reveal to Mike her mother's worry over Chris, perhaps this moment could be the right time she contemplated. So during their meal said 'Mike I need to talk to you about a particular issue which has been worrying my mother, I hope you won't mind'. 'Not at all Jess, what is it?'

Jess, therefore, relayed to Mike her mother's concern. At the same time apologised most sincerely for allowing this to intrude on their lovely time together. Of course sweet Mike understood and took in every word Jess relayed. He wrote down in his notebook, which he always carried with him, the answers to his questions. Mike required his surname, what his job was and where he lived, also the school he went to. Jess wasn't able to answer all of his questions but said she would find out and let him know.

'Ok' said Mike as he put his notebook away 'please leave it with me and I'll endeavour to see if there is anything my team can do to find out more'. 'Thank you so much Mike, it's a relief for me to share my Mum's worried thoughts with you as I had no clue as to what to do to take away her concern'. 'Ok, now you've told me let's now concentrate on each other' said Mike.

On the way home Jess mentioned to Mike that she would like to introduce him to climate change at some stage as it was a most important issue. Jess was aware that he'd had very little thought on the subject. She only wished him to be aware and to think a little about it as it was a problem and one of her passions. Of course he agreed to have a session with her at some stage. Not now though he'd remarked with his thoughts on relatively lighter subjects.

At home Jess invited Mike in for a quick coffee before he departed. Both had to be up sharp and early the following morning for work so he did not stay too long.

Mike took Jess in his arms at the door as they said goodnight. He kissed her on the lips with a little passion and thanked her for sharing a wonderful day with him. Jess reciprocated his kiss and thanked him profusely too.

After Mike had left Jess sincerely hoped she hadn't disillusioned him when she'd mentioned her mother's worry about Chris and then her need for him to be aware of climate change. Oh had she been silly she pondered when they'd spent a most enjoyable day together.

It was rather late but Jess made a quick telephone call to her mother and requested Chris's personal details for Mike to do his best to help. Jess did not reveal the reason for such an appeal but simply said to trust her. Her mother agreed with a response that she would do her best to find out and get back to her.

Chapter 42

Monday morning came all too soon although Jess was so pleased to see her class of children who were always a delight. Also Jess was very happy after her delightful weekend spent with Mike.

'So children we're going to learn a little about Shakespeare today, a renowned English playwright, who was born a long while ago in 1564 in Stratford-upon Avon His birthday was on the 23rd April 1564 and he wrote many plays which are very famous today.

I think you are all a little young for me to read any of his plays to you. I would just like you to be aware of him and the many famous plays he wrote. I am sure one day when you are much older you will become more aware of Shakespeare as he remains very famous still today. So I will tell you a little about him.

William Shakespeare would have lived with his family in their house on Henley Street, Stratford until he reached the age of eighteen. He was only eighteen when he married Anne Hathaway, who was much older at twenty six. Together they had three children, a daughter and twin boys.

I would like you to write down the names of the plays he wrote in your exercise books when I tell you some of the titles in a moment'. Jess continued 'Shakespeare's reputation was established in London. He would leave Stratford for London on horseback. Can you imagine riding a horse nearly 100 miles to London. There would have been places for him to change his horse or the poor horse would have become extremely tired. London was where he wrote his most famous tragedies, such as "King Lear", and "Macbeth" as well as great romances, like "The Winter's Tale" and "The Tempest".

His comedies included "The Merchant of Venice" and "Much Ado About Nothing". Among his 10 history plays are "Henry V" and "Richard III".

Shakespeare altogether wrote 38 plays. His success in London made him very wealthy when he bought the largest house in his home town.

Shakespeare died on 23rd April 1616, his birthday, at the age of only 52 at his home in Stratford upon Avon'.

Jess finished the lesson with 'I think that's enough for you children. However, hopefully, when you get to Senior School and Shakespeare is brought up in a lesson you may be able to recall what Miss Aries taught you in Primary School'.

As this was part of their history lesson Jess was unsure as to whether or not the children were that interested. She felt they were indeed rather young to absorb this short history on Shakespeare. Hopefully some of it would be retained for their future.

It was very obvious to Jess that Tommy seemed a lot happier and was now not falling asleep in class, especially when the lesson could be rather boring for some.

Jess had no further lessons for the rest of the day which allowed her to take time out in the Staff Room to work on her next lesson for the children.

Claire popped into see Jess on her way home from work as they'd not seen each other for a number of days.

Sat down together over a cup of tea, with a slice of Jess's delicious cake it was nice to catch up. 'Come on Claire, we've missed each other for various reasons, what's happened with you and Adrian?'

'Oh Jess I've really enjoyed seeing more of Adrian and we seem so happy when we're together'.

'Oh I'm so pleased for you Claire, tell me more, is he all that you hoped he might be away from his busy work?'

'Jess he's so kind and caring, he makes me feel we've been dating for months. I've been out with him a few times now and we've arranged to go out for the day somewhere when he's not on call. I really like him Jess and I believe he is keen on me too'. Jess gave Claire a huge hug and told her how delighted she was to hear her good news. 'Keep me posted won't you?' said Jess. 'Of course' Claire retorted.

Mike telephoned shortly after Claire's departure. He asked how Jess was and how her day had been and Jess enquired about his day too which had been uneventful for once, he remarked.

'Mum's given me Chris's details already' said Jess and proceeded to pass Mike the information he required. 'Gosh that was quick. 'Ok, please try not to worry and I'll see what we can possibly find out for you'.

Jess expressed how grateful she was for anything Mike could do. They each passed a few pleasantries and rang off with the final words of let's get together soon. So pleased to hear him speak that way at last, Jess felt perhaps it was going to work between them after all.

Chapter 43

Mike gave two of his team members, Bob and Nick, the information on Chris passed to him by Jess. 'Do your best to observe this young man when and where feasible' he directed.

It would be an easy surveillance task for them after they'd located Chris's home address. Rather tedious and boring until Chris eventually is spotted. Bob and Nick have his appearance details so are pretty sure they'd identified him. They followed from a distance as he drove off.

Chris had gone about his work duties as a Surveyor with a colleague, the guys presumed, which evidently proved rather innocent.

Bob and Nick hung around for over a week and reported back to HQ that there was nothing untoward with their observation up to now.

The job had become relatively monotonous for them by this time, as they stretched their legs in turn. Chris seemed to do his job as usual, met up with a girl, presumably Holly. Both are watched as they pop into a Café briefly and depart company shortly after.

Nick again relayed this information from his intercom to HQ for Mike. 'Still nothing untoward so far' was his short message. Mike is busy but they receive a message from Dan to continue their surveillance. Over the next couple of days they do just that.

Suddenly, Bob had become aware that Chris, who apparently had just arrived home from work, was waylaid by a guy who seemed somewhat aggressive towards him. Chris looked shaken and behaved in a somewhat subservient manner then he placed his right hand upon his forehead with a shake of his head. Apparently reluctant to do what was asked of him.

A packet was detected handed over and fairly obvious to Bob and Nick that Chris was very reluctant to take it. However the package appeared to be forced upon him by the guy who maybe was foreign with his dark complexion and appearance.

Of course this was surveyed from a distance so maybe they're wrong, but didn't believe so. Bob and Nick are experienced men on Mike's team and rarely mistaken.

Bob did not take his eyes off of them while Nick made contact with HQ and managed to relay this back to Mike. 'Ok', said Mike in reply 'this may, of course, be innocent but Nick you follow this chap and Bob to politely question Chris inside his home and get back to me'. 'Right, Sir' Nick confirmed.

Bob, as he'd heard Mike's request, quick as a flash removed himself from the car which enabled Nick to pursue the suspect as he walked towards his car.

Chris home alone answered the door to Bob's knock. Bob, at once, noticed the anxious look on his face before he showed his police identification. When he does so 'may I come in' Bob requested.

Rather reluctant Chris had no choice and agreed. Bob first of all asked a few general questions to relax Chris. He, of course, is unsure as to whether Bob's police identification is genuine. Therefore is disinclined to answer simple questions. Bob is smart and is aware of this and reassured him of his authority.

Eventually Chris is asked to identify the contents of the package handed over to him. At first he is unwilling to do so but Bob is insistent, albeit in a very calm manner as instructed.

The package is therefore opened and Bob is amazed to witness the many illegal drugs contained within. Bob then asked for an explanation, but remarked that he would record on his mobile recorder everything he had to say. Even more nervous and with tears in his eyes Chris endeavoured to reveal his story.

'I was a young 13 year old boy when a man offered me pocket money if I delivered a package to someone not far from my school, so it was within easy walking distance.

This would happen frequently but I was happy to do so for the pocket money, which wasn't very much, but a lot for me at the time.

When I left school I refused to continue to deliver these packages with no idea of what was contained in them. However, as I matured guessed it was something illegal.

Not only was I threatened with my life but my parents and sister's too. I had no idea who to turn to so when approached, I continued to deliver them, but refused to accept any money for doing so'.

Bob switched off his machine. 'Thank you Chris, you're not in any trouble but I'd like you to accompany me to HQ, is that ok with you?' 'I'm not sure' said Chris in reply 'I'm really nervous if this particular guy, I believe his name is Mo, finds out'. 'Don't be alarmed Chris we'll take care of you and the situation'.

With that Bob called HQ for a car to pick them up and transport them as, of course, Nick was on the chase.

At the same time Nick had followed the supposed perpetrator, made contact with HQ as to his whereabouts and continued with his observation.

At HQ Mike did not wish to reveal himself, when Bob entered with Chris, due to his friendship with Jess, the sister of his supposed friendship with Holly. Mike, therefore, viewed the proceedings from the Observation Room after he'd arranged with his assistant Dan to receive Chris with Bob when they arrived.

Now with confirmation that this was a criminal activity, Mike made contact with Nick again with a further update of the present situation and for him to persevere with his surveillance. To call immediately if he required back-up support. 'Ok, but nothing sinister as yet Sir' was Nick's response.

Chris is introduced to Dan who sat and listened to the tape bearing Chris's explanation recorded by Bob. 'Is there anything you may wish to change?' asked Dan. Chris shook his head with a very quiet 'No'.

Nick, at the same moment, was on a very urgent call to Mike 'the suspect I've followed has picked up three more males and I believe are headed towards Kidston Airfield'. 'Good man, my guess is they're expecting a haul of drugs delivery from a light aircraft. Keep in touch Nick we'll be close at hand'. 'Ok Sir'.

Mike immediately organised members of his team to drive post haste to meet up with Nick surreptitiously at the stated Airfield. Spoke to Dan on his private intercom. 'Arrange for an officer to escort Chris home, explain he has nothing to fear.

181

If he is still agitated or concerned ask the officer to stay with him if Chris would prefer. Get back to me as quickly as you can Dan, we have a job to do'.

Mike and Dan meet up with Nick, who is well hidden from the four men who appear to await the arrival of an impending aircraft. The others from HQ are also well hidden in a police van.

In the distance the sound of an aircraft is heard. As it approached the runway and came to a halt. The four individuals race over to the plane with a trolley. A great many fairly large boxes are handed over by the pilot.

'Not a lot we can do about them at the moment' said Mike 'evidently foreign from appearance, write down any identification mark you may be able to see on the aircraft Dan. We'll try and get HQ to follow it up for us'.

Mike made contact with a driver of one of the police vans and informed him to take four officers with him, and he and Dan would follow the suspects to wherever they intend to make their delivery and for the police officer to follow Mike's unmarked car.

The suspects eventually pull up before a gated rather salubrious mansion type property. 'This is not going to be easy, we need to catch them all red-handed' said Mike. Dan agreed with a slightly concerned expression.

One of the police officers in the van, Mike is well aware, was extremely athletic spoke to the said officer on the intercom. 'Cliff do you think you could do your best to get inside the gated property in a clandestine manner?' Cliff is keen to oblige and knew exactly what was required without being told.

The team are anxious as they await unseen nearby when Cliff made contact. He was now inside the premises and had discreetly found a way to observe their operation. Beforehand, he'd witnessed many boxes lifted from the car and taken into an adjacent building. He'd seen the boxes of presumably illegal drugs in the process of being checked.

'Right we're coming in' Mike retorted. 'We don't wish to alarm them but clearly need to catch them in the act'. Cliff explained that the building being used was next to the large house.

Mike and Dan drove to the property and with a special device opened the gates and were made to remain open for the police van when called. Once inside Mike and Dan decide to park their car and go on foot to the building in order not to disturb the suspects. Also they're sure they could possibly be seen via a CCTV camera which was more easily avoided on foot.

Cliff spotted them and with a hand signal beckoned and pointed to where the suspects are. As Cliff had witnessed in advance thousands of drugs laid out and displayed, Mike and Dan burst in with guns at the ready. The men looked up totally surprised and confused and immediately were inclined to lash out but Mike and Dan simultaneously drew their guns and told them to step back and sit down and then showed their police identification.

Cliff with a signal from Mike called the police van driver who entered the property with Cliff's direction.

'You are all under arrest for the illegal possession of dangerous drugs for onward sale'. Before any of the traffickers can escape they're all handcuffed and marched off to the waiting police van which is large enough to accommodate all of them.

It is hoped that they will eventually be given hefty jail sentences to take these evil characters off the streets for the safety of law abiding citizens and young vulnerable children. HQ would continue to search for the mastermind behind this particular gang and others too which, of course, would take some time.

This is a job well done as organised crime groups involved in drug trafficking are typically also involved in a range of criminal activities. The profits of illegal drugs are used to fund other forms of criminal operations, including buying illegal firearms and financing terrorism.

Crime associated with drug trafficking is very often violent, with the direct links to the criminal use of firearms and gang feud knife attacks, together with exploitation of young and vulnerable people.

Chapter 44

Within a very short time Mike caught up with Jess by telephone as he was rather desperate to put her mind at rest with regard to her sister Holly's boyfriend.

'Hi Jess, we've done an investigation and I want to reassure you that there is no need for you, your mother or, indeed, Holly to be concerned about Chris.

However Mike was not in a position to notify Jess of the details as this was a drug trafficking police investigation. Also it would be up to Chris himself if ever he wished to reveal to the family his innocent connection with these villains, not Mike.

'Thank you so much Mike for what you've done, whatever it was. Mum will be relieved as she, most probably was barking up the wrong tree'. 'No Jess she was right to be concerned but do call her and I would suggest she might do her best to be hospitable, kind and friendly towards Chris'.

'Yes, ok' said Jess but this led her to believe there was more to this than met the eye but asked no questions as she trusted Mike implicitly. If he wished to reveal more to her that would be up to him.

Mike did not divulge anything further about the investigation but ended their short conversation with 'I'll call you on Friday evening if that's ok with you Jess?' 'Yes, ok that will be fine'. With a cheery goodbye Jess replaced the receiver.

Jess had had several very short conversations with her mother since their telephone call about her concerns in regard to Chris. Unfortunately Jess had been unable to instantly help with her mother's anxiety.

Now with the information Jess had received from Mike she could relay this to her and, hopefully, put her mother's mind at rest.

'Hi Mum, I have some information for you with regard to Chris and it's fairly good news. I can reassure you there is no reason for you to worry about him. He is not a drug addict, so please try to be friendly and hospitable towards him'.

'Well that's a relief Jess but why are you telling me this, and what has made you so sure?'

'Mum I don't know any more than I've told you. However, I think it's time for you to know I have been dating Mike who is with the CID. I have known him for some time but only very recently have we become an item.

I gave Mike the details you gave to me on Chris and he organised an investigation. He was not at liberty to divulge more to me and I had no right to question him.

All I can say is I'm sure he and his team did a thorough analysis. I've not the vaguest idea what was found out or, indeed, how this conclusion was reached. The only thing we need to know is Chris is in the clear'.

'Well that's a load off my mind Jess. No further questions and I'm sure Dad will also be relieved. It would be very nice to meet Mike at some stage. I'm sure he is very busy, as you are, but please try to visit before too long'.

'Yes Mum, of course, I'll do my best to make it happen. As you say, we are very busy but happy. I hope he's the one for me Mum'. 'Really Jess, well let's see. As I said it would be so nice to meet him and look forward to seeing you soon. Bye for now love'. 'Bye Mum'.

Jess truly hoped her message would have put a wee smile upon her mother's face.

Jess and Mike had managed to meet up, when work permitted, fairly often even though he, of course, was on call day and night. Both comfortably relaxed at Jess's home after a meal they'd happily cooked together, when they were disturbed by his police intercom for him to be called away in an emergency.

They had been in the process of discussing Mike's home, a couple of miles away from Jess, and that it was about time he took her for a visit also when would be most convenient for them both and then he was called away.

'I'm more than sorry Jess, have to go, I'll call you later if I can or tomorrow morning first thing'. 'Whatever it is, please be careful' said Jess. 'Don't you worry sweetheart, I'm used to this' he retorted. With a hurried kiss goodbye Mike dashed off.

As Jess closed the door, she felt so warm inside at the thought of him as he called her sweetheart for the first time. Their friendship had taken a long while to begin to blossom and to reach this point. At long last Jess was now so terribly happy and truly hoped he would be safe whatever the emergency he'd been called out for.

Jess spent rather a restless night in the end as Mike had not managed to call and again hoped with all her heart that he was okay and safe.

Mike rang first thing in the morning and apologised profusely for not having called her late last night to put her mind at rest but he was fine.

'How about I pick you up later this morning, we have lunch at my place and I show you around my abode. Then afterwards would you like me to give you a driving lesson. We could start off at a disused airstrip which is near to my place?' Oh my goodness Jess thought before replying 'that would be wonderful Mike, but I hope you won't be too disappointed with my first attempt'. 'We all have to make a start sometime Jess'.

Jess met him at the door with a hug, so grateful to see him in one piece after being called away at short notice. 'What happened?' Jess enquired as she took him by the hand and ushered him into the lounge.

'Oh I was needed to interrogate a terrorist suspect rather urgently and I happened to be the nearest and most senior CID officer. Dan, my assistant, could have dealt with it, but I was geographically closer to HQ'.

Now ready to leave and within 15 minutes or so had arrived at Mike's home. Jess noticed the quiet and salubrious neighbourhood when he pressed in a code number for the large gates to open. Jess was so impressed but said nothing.

Mike first of all showed her around, gosh his home was so palatial Jess thought. Three bedrooms, two bathrooms, a living room and a separate dining room all beautifully decorated. This was the lap of luxury was her further thought but knew not to gasp in wonder. Finally, Mike walked her through to the Conservatory where they sat down together with a drink and sandwich Mike had previously prepared. Now Jess could absorb his stunning home.

Although secretly in love with Mike, Jess had not, as yet, expressed such words to him, and although his house was utterly amazing Jess felt she could live in a tent she cared so deeply for him.

A short time later he took her for her debut drive around the disused airstrip. 'Well I'm very impressed, you didn't appear to need much instruction'. 'Well maybe that's because I'd always witnessed my Dad at the wheel many times as I was growing up and before I left home' said a gleeful Jess.

Just a few days later and alone one evening Jess telephoned her mother. 'Hello Mum, how are you, do you have any news about Holly?' 'I'm fine Jess I do hope you're not working too hard' were her mother's first words.

'Well Mum a teacher always has so much prep to do, but I love it especially as I have the most delightful children in my class'.

'I do have some news for you' her mother began, 'first of all with all that's been going on we, myself and Holly, failed to let you know that she'd been positively selected to sing in the Musical Les Miserable which, of course, she accepted almost immediately. She will be singing "On My Own" from Les Mis. I wanted to reveal this to you at once. I felt badly that we hadn't let you know before now, although Holly hasn't known herself that long'.

'Oh Mum that's amazing news, please congratulate her for me. Perhaps when she's not so busy we can have a chat together'.

'Yes I'll tell her Grace responded 'I'm sure you would like to know that Holly brought Chris back for coffee a couple of nights ago. He'd been to rehearsals with her. I believe she persuaded him to help with the lighting as Chris is very good with electrics. Well what a difference in the young man. I really could not believe he was the same person, most cheerful, relaxed and caring particularly towards Holly, I was so pleased'.

Grace was pretty certain Jess's friend Mike had something to do with his changed demeanour, but, of course couldn't be certain. 'Please come for dinner as soon as you can' Grace reiterated 'and bring Mike along too, I would love to meet him. Just let me know in advance'.

Jess told her mother that she would be delighted to see her soon and to stay for dinner, and would bring Mike along to meet the family. Also, she mentioned how very pleased she was to hear the good news about Chris and extremely proud of Holly and really looked forward to seeing her in the show. Their conversation finished with the usual love and care. Jess thought Mike would be pleased to hear the difference in Chris, relayed by her mother, which she must convey to him soon as possible.

Not too long after their conversation, Jess was excited and happy to explain to Mike the difference her mother had seen in Chris. He appeared so much more relaxed and far happier. He was, naturally, most pleased to hear this splendid news and hoped to meet Chris when they went to Jess's home for dinner, which she'd passed the invitation on to him at the same time.

Chapter 45

At this time Jess wished desperately to introduce her lovely Mike to climate change as she was terribly worried about the planet.

If they eventually ended up together, married with children, which she desperately hoped, it would be the worry of them and their children who would bear the consequences.

However, she did not wish to spend their precious time together lecturing him but thought of a better idea.

With an evening free, Jess typed up some very brief basic notes on climate change problems for him and hoped he would take the opportunity to read and understand the problem. A worry and concern for each and every human being, or at least, it should be.

Most probably Mike's head was full of unlawful citizens creating havoc around the country, seeking them out and putting them behind bars for their wicked crimes, therefore, protecting the law abiding public.

This, hopefully, would be less stressful for him to read in the short term, albeit a future global crisis rather than the criminals he and his team imminently had to deal with.

Mike and Jess are somehow able to spend more time with each other as they have become more affectionately involved. One evening after a lovely romantic table setting for a meal together Mike was about to depart for home when Jess opened up about climate change.

'I hope you're up for this Mike but I've typed up some brief notes for you about my passion and what's happening to our world. Please try and find the time to cast your eye over them, if only to please me, but I really would like you to become aware'.

As she looked at the quizzical look Mike gave her Jess hoped she hadn't put a damper on their delightful evening. 'For you Jess I will do my best to read your notes and let you know what I think. On a more pleasant note why not come over to my place again and I cook dinner for you – well maybe cook something between us in my kitchen this time'. Let's make a date for some time next week. What do you think?' 'That would be great Mike, I would really like that'. Her private thought, his kitchen was far larger and could be rather fun to make a meal between them and a chance to work out all his mod-cons. The notes were handed over to him after a passionate goodnight kiss.

Mike was not overly enamoured as he took them from her but felt he must as he was actually falling in love with Jess. He started to read them that very night before he switched off his bedside light.

'Wild Weather is Worse to Come?'

'Destructive forest fires, torrential rain and fatal floods with temperatures that have shattered previous records, it's been a summer of severe global weather which is not over yet. However, what is causing these most serious occurrences?

These extreme events are basically impossible without climate change. How bad is it going to get? We're looking at a 5 fold increase in these type of events.

It's not just about far off disasters. The latest science predicts the UK is already undergoing disruptive climate change. Some residents are facing the threat on their doorstep with major floods. Is there worse to come?

Climate change is already affecting many regions on earth in multiple ways.

June 30th in Western Canada, a young man is hiding from a wild fire bounding towards him faster than he can run. He took shelter in the only place he could think of that will not burn, the gravel by the train tracks.

Driven by 70 kilometre an hour winds, the fire is spreading so fast it has already destroyed several homes before evacuation orders could even be sent. The fire destroyed 90% of the town of Lytton on Canada's West Coast.

The young man made it out alive but his home and livelihood are destroyed along with both of his parents who are killed.

The fire came after Lytton reported the hottest temperature ever recorded in Canada, 49.6°C. It is the kind of heat more often seen in Death Valley or the Sahara Dessert.

It is 5° above previous maximum recorded temperatures. These are approaching the sort of temperatures where humans really cannot survive.

This is the result of a high pressure weather system which settled over the region trapping hot air in what is known as a heat zone. It means temperatures are around 20° above average, also too in North Western USA.

On the other side of the Pacific homes are destroyed and cars overturned as more than 5 weeks of rain in 48hours caused devastating mud slides.

In New York, subways are overwhelmed with storm Elsa deluging the City with a month's average rainfall in just 24 hours.

Europe is waiting for extreme weather too. On the 10th July a Flood Researcher witnessed a flood alert on her system that something serious was going on. The European Flood Awareness System sent out an alert that a huge weather front had stalled over Germany making flooding very likely.

Despite the accurate forecast 4 days later scientists are stunned as they are confronted with the sense of utter devastation. At least 170 people in Germany and 36 in Belgium lost their lives by flash floods. Entire communities are ripped apart.

Around 15 centimetres of rain fell on July 14th, twice as much as usual for the entire month. This is absolutely terrible, we should not be seeing that number of people dying from floods in 2021.

Extreme floods continued throughout July. In China, 500 people were trapped in the underground as a year's rain fell in just 3 days, including a world record 20 centimetres in a single hour. 300 lost their lives.

As heat continues to build, an astonishing 5 zones with temperatures far in excess of normal form around the world, it leads to the worst month of wild fires in history.

Jonathan is in the midst of the biggest fire ever as it hits California. He is surrounded by flames and does not know if he will make it out alive. Jonathan escapes with his life, just.

By the end of July more than 40,000 fires have consumed 3 million acres of the USA. More than 1,000 homes have been destroyed and tens of thousands of people are forced to leave.

Tourist spots across the Mediterranean where more than 35,000 people do everything within their power to escape flames. The flames were watched as they approached the village of Mugla in Turkey. Villages were being wiped out.

Wild fires also raged in Italy, Algarve, Spain, France and Greece. 21 Firefighters from the UK were called in to dampen ground in Arcadia, South West of Athens to prevent the fire from spreading. August 11th in Sicily, Europe recorded its highest ever temperature 48.8°C.

United Nations IPCC reported that events we've seen during the summer could get worse.

Wild weather is not confined to far away shores anymore. We broke records in part of the UK this summer. We also had the country's first extreme heat warning. July 22nd Armagh, Northern Ireland hit 31.4°C breaking the record temperature for the third time that week. As they experienced blistering heat, hail stones, the size of golf balls, fell in Leicester.

Shortly after the worst flash floods in decades in London and the South East there is little let up. Just one week later in South Wales 100 millimetres of rain, more than a month's worth, fell in a single hour'.

What is triggering these events?

Some air pollution comes from natural sources but most result from human activity. Fossil fuels release greenhouse gases into the air. These emissions trap heat from the sun leading to a rise in global temperatures. This creates a cycle whereby air pollution contributes to climate and climate change creates higher temperatures. In turn higher temperatures intensify some types of air pollution.

Pollution is the introduction of harmful material into the environment. These harmful materials created by human activity such as rubbish or pollutants produced by factories damage the quality of air, water and land.

Cars spew pollutants from their exhaust pipes. Burning coal to create electricity pollutes the air.

Pesticides – chemical poisons used to kill weeds and insects – seep into waterways and harm wildlife.

All living things from one celled microbes to blue whales, depend on Earth's supply of air and water. When these resources are polluted, all forms of life are threatened.

As greenhouse gases trap more energy from the sun, the oceans are absorbing more heat, resulting in an increase in sea surface temperatures and rising sea levels. Rising sea levels caused by pollution and global warming means more dangerous weather with more powerful hurricanes, typhoons or cyclones.

Pollution is a global problem. For example, pesticides and other chemicals have been found in the Antarctic ice sheet. In the middle of the Northern Pacific Ocean a huge collection of microscopic plastic particles form what is known as the Great Pacific Rubbish Patch.

Rubbish fouls oceans. Many plastic bottles and other unwanted items are thrown overboard from boats which is a threat to fish and seabirds who mistake the plastic for food. Air and water currents carry pollution. Ocean currents and migrating fish carry pollutants far and wide.

When air pollutants mix with moisture, they change into acids and fall back to earth as acid rain. Acid rain can kill all forest trees. It can also devastate lakes, streams and other waterways. When lakes become acidic, fish cannot survive.

Greenhouse gases such as carbon dioxide and methane occur naturally in the atmosphere. In fact, they are necessary for life on Earth, preventing it from escaping into space. By trapping heat in the atmosphere, they keep Earth warm enough for people to live. This is called the greenhouse effect.

Human activities such as burning fossil fuels and destroying forests have increased the greenhouse gas effect, causing average temperatures across the globe to rise.

Global warming is causing ice sheets and glaciers to melt and the melting ice is causing sea levels to rise. Sea level rise poses a serious threat to coastal life around the world. Consequences include increased intensity of storm surges, flooding, and damage to coastal areas.

Global climate change has already had observable effects on the environment. Glaciers have shrunk, ice on rivers and lakes are breaking up earlier, plant and animal ranges have shifted and trees are maturing sooner.

Permafrost is often found in Arctic regions such as Greenland, Alaska, Russia, China and Eastern Europe. When permafrost is frozen, plant material in the soil, called organic carbon, cannot decompose, or rot away. As permafrost thaws, microbes begin decomposing this material. This process releases greenhouse gases like carbon dioxide and methane to the atmosphere.

Permafrost plays an essential role in the Arctic ecosystem by making the ground watertight and maintaining the vast network of wetlands and lakes across the Arctic tundra that provide habitat for animals and plants.

In the Northern Hemisphere, permafrost cover an estimated 9 million square miles

Just as permafrost locks in carbon and other greenhouse gases, it can also trap, and preserve, ancient microbes. It's believed that some bacteria and viruses can lie dormant for thousands of years in permafrost's cold, dark confines before waking up when the ground warms.

To help prevent permafrost from thawing, the everyday choices we make can contribute in some small way to climate change collectively which can add up to a big impact on the world's climes. By reducing our carbon footprint, investing in energy-efficient products, we can help preserve the world's permafrost and avert a vicious cycle of an ever-warming planet.

Effects that scientists had predicted in the past that would result from global climate change are now occurring: loss of sea ice, accelerated sea level rise and longer, more intense heat waves.

Scientists have high confidence that global temperatures will continue to rise for decades, largely due to greenhouse gases produced by human activity. The Intergovernmental Panel on Climate Change (IPCC), which includes more than 1,300 scientists from the United States and other countries, forecast a temperature rise of 2.5° to 10° Fahrenheit over the next century.

According to the IPCC, the extent of climate change effects on individual regions will vary over time and with the ability of different societies and environmental systems to mitigate or adapt to change.

The IPCC predicts that increases in global mean temperature of less than 1.8° to 5.4° Fahrenheit (1° to 3°)Celsius above 1990 levels will produce beneficial impacts in some regions and harmful ones in others. Net annual costs will increase over time as global temperatures increase.

Global climate is projected to continue to change over this century and beyond. The magnitude of climate change beyond the next few decades depends primarily on the amount of heat-trapping gases emitted globally, and how sensitive the Earth's climate is to those emissions.

'Terra Carta'

Weather related disasters should serve as a wake-up call.

A report from the United Nations panel on climate change warned of unprecedented global warming described as 'a code red' for humanity.

Terra Carta is a concept based on the 1215 Magna Carta with the aim to hold major companies accountable to help protect the planet.

Business leaders declare that genuine sustainability is not a fascination. It must inform and lie at the heart of all their business activities.

In view of the fact that we have been busily testing our world to destruction and left everything to the last minute, so that time is rapidly running out, they can only hope to win this epic battle if their counterparts in Governments work with them to create the right conditions for an accelerated green transition.

This is crucially important for our survival on this increasingly over-heating planet – something our children and grandchildren are rightly and deeply concerned about.

We have been testing our world to destruction. It is up to all citizens to become involved in an attempt to combat climate change.

As an example: We have witnessed devastating fires affecting Greece, Turkey and now Italy which has recorded Europe's highest ever temperature.

It is a nightmare to see the once blue skies above the Peloponnese Attica and the island of Evia turn a vivid orange as mile after mile of the country's landscape and over 100,000 hectares of forest and farmland have been swallowed up by ferocious flames causing tragic loss of life, injury and widespread destruction of homes and livelihoods.

Fires, floods and the increasingly severe droughts that have affected Australia make it very clear. Our planet is in crisis and, no matter where you are, no country is immune.

The predictions of the United Nation's report on climate change stated, scientists estimated there is an 89% chance of extreme events that used to occur once in a century happening every year.

We all need to do our bit right now to help combat climate change. As the UN Panel stressed, there is still time to do this, but only just.

The Sun gives our planet more energy than people use as fossil fuels, its heat always drives the engine of all the Earth's climate. It does not damage the Earth

Professor James Lovelock – 'How to Save Humankind'

He named the idea after the ancient Greek goddess of Earth – Gaia

Gaia is the name given to the system of organisms that lie on the earth that maintain its climate suitable for life.

However James Lovelock's Gaia is no kindly goddess protecting human kind from itself he argues that humans have pushed Gaia to its limit and whilst the Earth will eventually rebalance itself it may be too late for the human race unless humans start making drastic changes.

I wonder what your thoughts will be Mike when you get to the end of these notes. I cannot wait to hear your comments, whatever they may be.

Love Jess.

Chapter 46

Eventually, Mike had two days off and Jess quickly arranged with her mother to pay a visit at long last.

'We're so pleased to meet you Mike' as he and Jess are greeted at the door. Ted immediately heard their arrival and rushed forward to shake Mike by the hand and to hug his daughter.

This was the first time Mike had physically set eyes on Chris as they are ushered through to the lounge. Holly jumped up, 'how nice to meet you Mike, this is Chris' as he had quickly stood up beside her. Mike gave Holly a peck on the cheek and greeted Chris with a super handshake and 'great to meet you Chris' with a broad smile across his face.

Jess's family are extremely happy to meet Mike, especially Grace, as she is so certain he had something to do with the change in Chris. On the other hand he is extremely pleased to meet them all and, with his police training, observed Chris now and again to confirm his changed demeanour.

After a scrumptious roast lamb, with mint sauce, meal and glorious raspberry and apple pie for dessert during which everyone chatted together in a most friendly way, considering this was the first time the family had met Mike. He spoke directly to Holly about her singing in the show, how it was going and hoped against hope that he would be free to come to the show when they are given tickets with the date.

Time now for them to bid their farewells Mike's car is parked in their driveway so all four come outside to wave them off and hope to see them again very soon.

'What a lovely family you have' Mike said to Jess on the way home. He hadn't mentioned this to her before but went on to say he had a brother who lived in Australia and that both his parents had died in a road accident when he and his brother were teenagers. Jess squeezed his thigh and said how sorry she was to hear that. He went on to say that it had made a man of him as he'd had to stand on his own two feet from then on but he missed them dreadfully.

He missed his brother, Tom, too and looked forward to his visit to the UK with his wife next year. Jess responded that she would love to meet them and would look forward to their visit.

It was rather late when they arrived back at Jess's flat. As Mike did not have work the following day Jess asked if he would like to stay the night and said 'as you know I have two bedrooms so you will be quite safe'. Mike couldn't help but laugh at her comment but thought she was right to offer the spare room at this time which, fortunately, was already made up.

After a hot drink and a few comforting words and a wonderful goodnight kiss, they retired to their individual bedrooms.

Morning came all too soon Jess appeared to be awake first so she took a cup of tea into Mike. 'Good morning sweetheart' were his first words. 'Good morning' said Jess and pecked him on the cheek. She sat down on his bed to drink their cup of tea when Mike said 'as I don't have anything with me would you mind coming to my house after breakfast'. 'Of course' said Jess but please have a shower here first'.

With that Jess left the room to quickly prepare breakfast and within a short time they were on their way to Mike's home.

After Mike had done his shaving and what knot at his home he felt so comfortable with Jess and knew in his heart now must be the right time to reveal to her his past with Lucy. He, therefore, bravely opened up to her which Jess at once witnessed how traumatic this was for him.

Of course, unbeknown to Mike she knew a little of his life with Lucy revealed to her by Josie. This obviously enabled her to be more controlled and not so taken aback as when Jess had first learned about Lucy.

Jess listened intently to Mike's story, when he'd finished she noticed his eyes had welled up. Jess took him into her arms, held him tightly and said 'we will forever remember Lucy without her we would never have met'.

Mike with tears in his eyes which did not overflow hugged Jess with great emotion. 'Thank you' was his only word.

Later after he's recovered from the trauma of talking about Lucy Mike revealed that he'd read her notes on climate change.

'Jess your words were a real eye opener for me as I read your notes. I must be honest I was not at all in the least enthusiastic about reading them'.

'As you are aware, I had no idea about climate change. In fact I knew I was totally ignorant of the fact. My job has taken me into demanding and formidable depths at times so I guess climate change had not entered my head'.

Mike then revealed to Jess that her notes were a wake-up call for him. How proud he was of her, even more so now, not only for bringing these challenging, and devastating events to his notice, but for her passion to do her bit to help.

'Thank you Jess, I love you'. Jess was more than overwhelmed to hear those words from Mike, her tummy turned right over. She had realised she loved him too, but didn't wish to say so at this moment. However, she embraced him with a loving kiss and a thank you for now.

They had an exquisite and lovely day together with so much revealed and discussed between them when, eventually, they took a lovely walk in the meadow before a quiet lunch. Then later they made dinner together at Mike's before he took Jess home.

Chapter 47

It was about time Jess rang Josie as she so much wanted to give her an update of her blossoming relationship with Mike. One evening Jess rang her with the news. 'I thought as much as Jeff informed me that he had seen a far happier Mike when they'd met up in the Laboratory recently. Of course I'd told you that Jeff and I had been seeing rather a lot of one another and we're now so very happy together'. 'That's wonderful news Josie'.

Josie continued. 'Why don't we all meet up for dinner, the four of us, what do you think? 'If the guys are agreeable, I'd love to' said Jess. 'Ok let's make a tentative arrangement for next Saturday evening. I'll speak to Jeff and you to Mike and we'll plan to go to a very nice Restaurant. Between you and I Jess we'll secretly celebrate how happy we are, you with Mike and me with Jeff'. 'That sounds great Josie but don't you think that's a bit underhand'. 'Not at all my lovely girl, they are blokes not girlies like us, this will be a little secret between us celebrating our luck with a future, hopefully, with two extremely nice men, but Jess, remember, they are lucky to have found us too'.

'Ok Josie you're dead right, let's arrange it, we'll let each other know and hope Mike will be available'. With another few pleasantries they said their goodbyes.

So it was the following Saturday and so pleased Mike was free when Jess informed him that she was taking him out for dinner at a surprise Restaurant. Josie did the same and told Jeff but neither divulged that they would not be alone.

Jess could drive now with her lessons from Mike but still, unfortunately hadn't passed her test. Sadly that meant Mike would need to collect her from home and drive to an unknown destination which he agreed to do.

'This is all very mysterious' said Mike as he opened the car door for her. 'Really' said Jess as she guided him as to where to go. They arrived at a very high class Restaurant. Jess could see that Josie's car was already in the car park. She had obviously decided to drive which was one up on Jess and did not mention this to Mike as they walked through the entrance.

Greeted by the Maitre d and shown to a table for four. Mike immediately thought that a little odd. Josie and Jeff must have been at the bar so Josie suggested they have a drink first. This was so unlike Jess to behave in thus way were Mike's thoughts. Jeff and Josie pounced on them as they walked to the Bar. What a wonderful foursome they made as they so happily greeted each other and had a drink together before sitting at their table.

'Now I understand how secretive Jess has been' said Mike. 'I was beginning to get a little worried but I'm so glad to see you both'. Jeff announced that Josie had been equally secretive especially when she insisted on driving'.

Josie and Jess announced 'this is our treat guys so just enjoy'. Josie gave Jess a little wink as they sat down together at the table.

A most enjoyable evening was spent when at the end of their meal Jeff declared that he had asked Josie for her hand in marriage and she had accepted. Jess was blown away as her best friend had kept this from her. Of course she couldn't drink too much in celebration as she was driving.

Deep congratulations were conveyed to them. 'You crafty pair, you kept that very quiet' said Jess. 'Well I only asked her before we left'. Now Jess could understand why Josie hadn't said as she'd only known herself a short time ago.

Well they had much to celebrate and after a scrumptious meal and lots to say it was time to leave the Restaurant with lots of kisses and hand-shakes with 'see you fairly soon'.

'Well what a surprise that was' said Mike as they motored home. 'I'll say' Jess remarked 'I was so surprised but I'm pleased for them as they both seem so very happy'. Mike agreed wholeheartedly, popped in with Jess and thanked her implicitly for the lovely surprise meal with the other two. Jess made a quick hot drink before he left with 'call you tomorrow'

At last Jess received a telephone call from Holly. 'Jess I'm truly sorry please forgive me for not making contact before now'. 'Yes I forgive you but at last I can give you my personal congratulations. I understand from Mum you're singing "On My Own" from Les Mis'.

'Yes, I'm going to put in the post some tickets for you. I'm sure you'd like to bring Josie and Claire along'. 'Indeed I would Holly but I would be more than happy to purchase some tickets too. I expect Mum mentioned that I'm seeing a lot of Mike and also Josie with Jeff too, not forgetting Claire with Adrian, that's six of us. However, my guess is they won't all be available on whichever night the tickets are for. Both Mike and Adrian always on call. Anyway we'll cross that bridge nearer the time'.

'Ok Jess I'll send you six tickets, check who will be free and I would be grateful for you to return any tickets that may not be used for the night in question and I can then pass them on'

'Thank you so much Holly, of course I will. Before you go, how are things with you and Chris?' 'Oh we're really great together, it took a little while at first but we seem more settled'. 'I'm really pleased to hear that' said Jess and with words 'look forward to seeing you', rang off.

Jess received the tickets from Holly for Les Mis which were for a Saturday evening in two weeks' time. Holly had explained to Jess that the original Les Mis was, of course, an exceedingly long and complicated story and that this show would be very much more condensed so don't expect too much Holly warned in her note attached.

Mike and Jess took their seats with Claire, Josie and Jeff. Unfortunately Adrian couldn't make it as he had a Paediatric emergency.

My goodness said Jess to Mike as Holly had ensured that her sister and friends would have very good seats in the Stalls not quite in the front but in the middle centre which gave them an amazing view.

Jess and Josie knew Les Mis pretty well as they'd gone to London in their student days especially to see this particular Musical. The girls could see that it had been adapted considerably but Jess was so proud of Holly who not only sang "On My Own" but two other songs from the show. "I Dreamed a Dream" then at the very end "Bring Him Home".

Mike looked at Jess and could see the tears as they fell down her cheeks and lovingly squeezed her hand. Josie too was in tears unable to look at Jess for fear of them both crying uncontrollably.

They were invited back stage briefly to congratulate Holly and then, surprisingly, were offered a small glass of wine. The Director obviously enchanted with Holly's performance as Jess and her friends were too.

'What a wonderful experience that was' said Mike on their way home. 'Your sister has the most exquisite voice and so right for that Musical'. Jess agreed wholeheartedly with her own words of praise for Holly.

Mike did not take Jess back to her flat but drove to his own home. 'I hope you won't mind and not think it rather presumptuous of me but I would like you to spend the night with me at my place'.

Jess's stomach gave a lurch as this was so unexpected. 'I don't have anything with me Mike' were her frantic words. 'Don't you worry about that, I have catered for your needs sweetheart'. Her immediate thought was he must have planned this, like tit for tat for not letting on about the secret dinner with Josie and Jeff but didn't mind at all, in fact rather looked forward to it.

Mike was magically entertaining before he showed her to the en suite bedroom. A little disappointed at not asked to share his room but, thought, maybe next time.

However as he'd explained, all her needs were catered for – pyjamas, a pair of his, laid out on the bed and many assorted creams in the bathroom. She closed her eyes for sleep with thoughts of, what an amazing man.

Chapter 48

Monday morning came all too soon after an exciting time spent with Mike at his home.

Jess had repeatedly kept a surreptitious eye on young Tommy and recently had witnessed a positive change in him

He did not appear so isolated from the other children and was joining in with them during playtime. Jess had noticed him laughing at times which cheered her heart and felt she must discreetly ask him what had brought about this supposed happy change in him.

When the time was appropriate, Jess called Tommy over to her desk at the end of the school day. 'How are you Tommy?' questioned Jess. 'Alright, Miss' he responded. 'Can you tell me what has made you feel happier Tommy?' 'Well miss it was the poem you gave to me and every night before I go to sleep I try to read it'.

'That is really good for you to do that Tommy, so what was it about the poem that helped you to be happy? 'I think it was the bit that my Mummy couldn't be with me but wanted me to be happy for her and that would make her happy'.

Jess had to struggle not to weep in front of Tommy as he expressed these words but said, with his hands in hers 'I'm so very proud of you Tommy and I'm sure you feel much better now you know Mummy can keep her eye on you'. Tommy replied with a smile 'yes miss'. 'Off you go young Tommy but please remember to come and talk to me after lessons if you'd like to'.

Tommy nodded with a smile and skipped off. Jess watched as he disappeared from view. She'd wanted desperately to give him a hug, but was so happy to see the change in him and prayed it would continue.

Jess had been given the task of organising the Nativity Play for this year and thought this a rather daunting prospect. Nevertheless, it's only as hard as you make it, she scolded herself. After all, these are children, you're going to stage a simple children's play not attempting to win an Oscar.

The first thing Jess did was make a list of actions:

1. Find a script
2. Audition a cast and understudies
3. Organise rehearsals
4. Prepare Costumes
5. Arrange help from Teachers and Parents

Oh my goodness, I would have loved all my spare time with Mike instead of so much of my time organising a Nativity Play. However he is, of course, extremely busy and always on call with his job anyway were Jess's thoughts. .

As soon as the right moment occurred, Jess managed to pull in a few teachers to assist with this impending mission while she took a break in the Staff Room. She breathed a sigh of relief at not having to carry this load alone. If she didn't have Mike to think about, she would have all the time in the world

Jess is keen to start her plan for the children's Nativity. Her class would be playing a major role and she was determined that young Tommy, who had been so brave, must be given a special part.

However, before Jess becomes too deeply involved with her plans, she and Mike discuss taking a week's leave together. She, therefore, arranged with Dora Orchard for Angus Smith, the supply teacher who her children are most comfortable with, to take her class for the week.

Mike, on the other hand, had no doubt that his assistant, Dan, would love to have complete control of all CID officers for the week.

As their relationship had grown much stronger they now looked forward to some very special time together without work commitments getting in the way. They had expressed their love for each other and Mike had taken her in his arms and indicated that he hoped one day Jess would move in with him, when the time was right, in other words very soon.

It was Sunday morning with the birds chirping and singing away Jess and Mike with no imminent work commitments walked so happily hand in hand through the meadow breathing in the crisp morning air. The colourful leaves as they fell from the trees left a carpet of colour for them as they walked into their future together.

BIBLIOGRAPHY

[1]* The Elephant and the Ant : Bill Peet
[1]* Ibiza Holiday : Catherine Bray
[1]* London Cycle Ride : Catherine Bray
[1]* My Planet : Oxford Ransackers 2006
[1]* David Attenborough
[1]*John Humphries : plastic bags and climate change
Climate Change – internet research
Personal Stories : Tsunami – 26th December 1904 : Indian Ocean
[1]* Mark Zimmerman family - Mart Oberle
[1]* Rosie – Emma Pengelly
[1]* Tom and Arlette Sttuip – Khao Lak, Thailand
[1]* A couple snorkelling on Koh Phi Phi
[1]* Edie - Kayaking - Dominic Horst, Special Correspondent
[1]* Sal Bini and family – Indonesia – David Jones, Newspaper Representative

Printed in Great Britain
by Amazon

68550713R00122